S0-BEQ-857

HARLEQUIN®
Presents

At Harlequin Presents we are always interested in what you, the readers, think about the series. So if you have any thoughts you'd like to share, please join in the discussion of your favorite books at www.iheartpresents.com—created by and for fans of Harlequin Presents!

On the site, find blog entries written by authors and fans, the inside scoop from editors and links to authors and books. Enjoy and share with others the unique world of Presents— we'd love to hear from you!

MISTRESS TO A MILLIONAIRE

*She's his in the bedroom,
but he can't buy her love…*

Showered with diamonds, draped in exquisite
lingerie, whisked around the world
in the lap of luxury…

The ultimate fantasy becomes a reality.

Live the dream with more
MISTRESS TO A MILLIONAIRE
titles by your favorite authors.

Available only from Harlequin Presents®.

Abby Green

BOUGHT FOR THE FRENCHMAN'S PLEASURE

MISTRESS
TO A
MILLIONAIRE

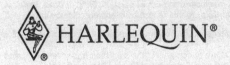

HARLEQUIN®

TORONTO • NEW YORK • LONDON
AMSTERDAM • PARIS • SYDNEY • HAMBURG
STOCKHOLM • ATHENS • TOKYO • MILAN • MADRID
PRAGUE • WARSAW • BUDAPEST • AUCKLAND

ISBN-13: 978-0-373-23485-1
ISBN-10:   0-373-23485-6

BOUGHT FOR THE FRENCHMAN'S PLEASURE

First North American Publication 2008.

www.eHarlequin.com

Printed in U.S.A.

All about the author…
Abby Green

ABBY GREEN deferred doing a social anthropology degree to work freelance as an assistant director in the film and TV industry— which is a social study in itself! Since then it's been early starts, long hours, mucky fields, ugly car parks and wet-weather gear—especially working in Ireland. She has no bona fide qualifications but could probably help negotiate a peace agreement between two warring countries after years of dealing with recalcitrant actors.

After discovering a guide to writing romance one day, she decided to capitalize on her long-time love for Harlequin romances and attempt to follow in the footsteps of such authors as Kate Walker and Penny Jordan. She's enjoying the excuse to be paid to sit inside, away from the elements. She lives in Dublin and hopes that you will enjoy her stories.

You can e-mail her at abbygreen3@yahoo.co.uk.

This is especially for Margaret, Peter, Jack and Mary B…not family by blood, but my family in every other conceivable way.

CHAPTER ONE

As Romain de Valois approached the ballroom he was glad for a second that the doors were closed. They acted as a barrier of sorts between him and that world. The thought caught him up short. *A barrier?* Since when had he ever thought he needed that? His strides grew longer, quicker, as if to shrug off the unaccustomed feeling that assailed him. And the most curious sensation hit him too at that moment…the desire to have someone by his side as he approached this set of doors. Someone…*a woman*…with her hand in his, who would understand effortlessly what he was thinking, who would glance up at him, a gleam of shared understanding in her eyes. She might even smile a little, squeeze his hand…

His steps faltered for just a second before reaching the door. The vibration of the orchestra, the muted raucous chatter and laughter of the hundreds of people inside was palpable in his chest. What on earth was wrong with him? Daydreaming about a woman when he'd never felt the lack of anything before—much less a *partner*. And one thing was for sure: no woman existed like that in his world, or even in his imagination until that second. If he wanted a woman like that he'd be better off going back to his small French home town, and he'd left that behind a long time ago—physically, mentally and emotionally. His hand touched the handle of the door, concrete and real, *not* like the disturbing wispy images in his head. He turned it and opened the door.

The rush of body heat, conversation, the smell of perfume mixed with aftershave was vivid and cloying. And yet there was a slightly awed hush that rippled through the room when he walked in. He barely noticed it any more, and wondered if he would even care if it didn't happen. His mouth twisted with unmistakable cynicism as his eyes skipped over the looks and the whisperings, seeking out his aunt. The fact was, as head of the fashion world's most powerful business conglomerate, he practically owned every single person who had anything to do with fashion in this huge glittering ballroom, and even some of those who rode on their coat-tails.

He owned all the dresses and suits so carefully picked out with a mind to current trends. He owned the ridiculously expensive cosmetics that sat on the flawless skin of the women, and the lustrous jewels that adorned their ears, necks and throats. They knew it and he knew it.

The crowd shifted and swayed to let him through, and for the first time in his life he didn't feel any kind of thrill of anticipation. In fact what he felt was…dissatisfaction.

He was relatively young, wealthier than any other man there, and he knew with no false conceit that he was handsome. Most important of all, he was single. And here in New York that put a bounty on his head. So he was under no illusions as to what he represented to women in a crowd like this. And those women he'd have taken his pick from before seemed now to be too garish, too accessible. Dismayingly, the ease with which he knew he could pick the most beautiful, the most desirable, now made distaste flavour his mouth. A pneumatic blonde dressed in little more than a scrap of lace held together by air bore down on him even now.

Relief flooded him when he saw his aunt, and he crossed to her side. Focusing on her brought his mind back to the reason he was there at all tonight. To check someone out in a professional capacity—a model he was being advised to hire for one of the most lucrative ad campaigns ever. His aunt was the latest to put pressure on him as the woman in question was one of her own models. He knew well that this woman, Sorcha Murphy, would be like every other in this room. And on top of that she had a history that made her, as far as he was concerned, unemployable. Still, though, he worked and operated his business as a democracy and had no time for despotic rule. He had to play the game, show that he had at least come to inspect her for himself before telling them no…

His aunt turned and smiled fondly in acknowledgment as he approached.

'No.' Sorcha took in a deep patient breath. 'It's pronounced Sor*ka*…'

'That's almost as cute as you, honey…and where is it from?'

The man's beady eyes set deep into his fleshy face swept up and down again with a lasciviousness that made Sorcha snatch her hand back from his far too tight and sweaty grasp. He clearly had no more interest in where she or her name were from than the man in the moon. She managed to say, with some civility and a smile that felt very fake, 'It's Gaelic. It means brightness…

It's been lovely meeting you, but if you wouldn't mind, I really must—'

'Sorcha!'

She looked around at her name being called with abject relief. The need to get away from this oily tycoon from Texas was acute and immediate.

'Kate…' She couldn't disguise that relief as she greeted her friend, and gave her a very pointed look.

Sorcha turned back to the man whose eyes were now practically popping out of his head as he saw the luminous blonde beauty join Sorcha's side. Her best friend merely smiled sweetly at him and led Sorcha away.

'Boy, am I glad to see you. I think I need a shower after that.' Sorcha gave a little shiver.

'I know. He cornered me earlier, and when I saw you with him I knew I had to save you.'

Sorcha smiled at her closest friend in the whole world and gave her a quick, impulsive hug. 'I'm so glad you're here, Katie. These evenings are such torture—do you think we could make a run for it?'

Kate's nose wrinkled in her exquisite face. 'No such luck. Maud is keeping her eagle eye on us, and has already told me that if we scarper early she'll make us pay.'

Sorcha groaned, and at that moment caught the eye of the woman in question—Maud Harriday, doyenne of the fashion industry and head of Models Inc, the agency in New York she and Kate worked for. And who was, for want of a better term, their surrogate mother.

She smiled sunnily until Maud's laser like gaze was distracted by something else, then stifled a huge yawn. They'd both been up since the crack of dawn for work that day, albeit for different catwalk shows.

Kate grabbed a passing waiter and took two glasses of champagne, handing one to Sorcha. She didn't normally drink the stuff but took it anyway, for appearances' sake. Maud liked her models to look as though they were enjoying themselves—especially when they were on show right in the middle of the mayhem of New York's Fashion Week in one of New York's finest hotels, rubbing shoulders with some of the most important people in media, fashion and politics.

Sorcha smiled and clinked glasses with Kate.

'Thanks. I always feel like some kind of brood mare at these functions…don't you?'

Kate was looking around with interest. 'Oh, I don't know, Sorch…' She affected the broad accents of Maud's famous New York drawl, and repeated her pep talk of earlier. '"This is the one time in the year we get to promote the new faces along with the old."' She nudged Sorcha playfully and said, *sotto voce*, 'At the grand age of twenty-five we're the old, in case you hadn't noticed…' She continued with her strident imitation. '"…and we generate business. These are the people who invest in you, the fashion advertisers who pay your bills, so go out there and look gorgeous."'

Sorcha threw back her head and laughed. 'She'd kill you if she heard you.'

The contrast of their beauty side by side—one blonde, the other dark—drew many gazes in their direction. They shared an easy intimacy that came from a long friendship that had started when Kate had gone to Sorcha's boarding school in Ireland, just outside Dublin.

Kate spoke again, bringing Sorcha's attention back from its wanderings. Her voice was deceptively light. 'Plenty of gorgeous guys here tonight, Sorch…'

A tightness came into Sorcha's face. She was recalling a recent heated discussion with her friend, and she had no desire to rake over the same ground now. No desire to go back down memory lane, where a comment like that was inevitably headed.

'Kate, let's not get into that again, *please*.' The entreaty in her clear blue eyes was explicit. Kate was her best friend—the one person who knew her like no other, who had seen her at her worst. The familiar guilt rose up, the feeling of debt. Even though she knew Kate would never mention it or use it against her. To her relief she saw her friend nod slightly.

'Ok, you're off the hook for now. But it's just…you are one of the most beautiful women I know, inside *and* out. I just wish—'

Sorcha took Katie's hand, halting her words. Her voice was husky. 'Thanks, Katie…but, really, just leave it for now—OK?'

It hadn't been hard to seek her out in the crowd. From her pictures alone she would have been easy to find, apart from the fact that she stood out effortlessly—a pale foil of beauty next to so much artifice and expensively acquired tan.

He watched the interplay between the two women covertly. He'd heard their laughter before he'd caught sight of her, and had been surprised to find that it had come from his quarry. It had floated across the room and wound its way around his senses. The sparkling smile was still on her face as she talked to her friend. He hated to admit it, but they weren't like the other models, fawning over the men in the crowd. They looked…like two children in the corner, playing truant. Bizarrely, because he wasn't given to such whims, it made him want to be a part of it…

She stood out in every possible way, with long wavy jet-black hair falling below her bare shoulders. In a strapless, high-waisted dress, the pale swell of her bosom hinted at a voluptuousness that was not usual for a top model, and her poise and grace screamed years of practice. The bluest of blue eyes were ringed by dark lashes, and he could see from across the room skin so pale he imagined that up close it would look translucent.

That niggle of dissatisfaction was coming back even stronger. Not usually given to any kind of introspection, Romain ruthlessly crushed it. Still watching the woman, he found his interest piqued beyond what he'd expected to be purely a quick professional once-over to confirm his own opinion…and even more so because she wasn't trying to capture his attention. His mouth compressed. That in itself was unusual.

He'd already decided he didn't want to use her…especially in light of her past notoriety…but, watching her now, he had to admit that on the face of it she would actually be perfect for what they were looking for. His instincts, honed over many years in the business, told him that in a second. Whether she'd contrived it or not, the smiling, sparkling animation on Sorcha Murphy's face effortlessly held his regard. Usually within these circles models were always so careful to put on some kind of front that any real expression had long been suppressed—either behaviourally or surgically.

He felt an almost overwhelming impulse to see her up close, and before he could control himself it had generated a throb of desire that wasn't usually prompted so arbitrarily. It was a response he couldn't control and which took him by surprise—*again.* It had been the last thing he'd expected to feel when faced with her.

'Beautiful, aren't they? I see that you've found her.'

He started at the low, husky voice that came from his right and was a little shocked at how enthralled he'd become. Had he been that obvious? He quickly schooled his face, but the woman beside him wasn't fooled, and he was thankful that he knew her well— that it was only she who had noticed his momentarily unguarded few seconds. His mouth quirked before he gave her a kiss on both cheeks, and she mock-fluttered her lashes.

'If I was still capable of blushing, my dear Romain, then I'd be red as a beetroot.'

'I'm sure,' he quipped dryly. She was at supreme ease in these gilded surroundings, and he couldn't imagine this veritable woman of steel blushing for anyone or anything.

'So…how are you, *ma chére tante*?'

She patted his cheek with her fan—a trademark eccentric accessory—and smiled affectionately. 'Very well, thank you. We are honoured to have a man of your calibre here. I'm so glad that for once our work interests have dovetailed so neatly as I never see you any more—although I don't imagine that the promise of a room full of beautiful women would have been any incentive?'

Romain tutted. 'First you flatter me, then you show what a low opinion you really have…'

'Hmm,' she said dryly. 'With pictures of you in numerous magazines courting what would appear to be every single model in Europe, I can see why you might want to seek out new pastures.'

He was used to this affectionate, teasing banter, though he would not have tolerated it in a million years from anyone else. He looked absently around the room. His aunt's words had hit their mark, and he had to curb a defensive desire to tell her exactly how long it had been since he *had* taken a lover. It didn't sit well with him to admit that even that area of his life seemed to be suffering.

Yet Sorcha Murphy stayed in his peripheral vision. It unnerved him, forcing him to say lightly, 'Now, you of all people should know that you can't believe everything you read in the press.'

'I don't know how you keep managing to generate all those billions of yours when you hardly seem to have the time. Always wining and dining—'

'Maud…' he said warningly, but in a completely unconscious gesture his eyes flicked away briefly to seek out Sorcha again. His aunt couldn't fail to notice.

'Ah, yes… So, what do you think?'

He shrugged nonchalantly. 'I'm still not sure…'

Sometimes the older woman was far too shrewd for her own good. And she knew him too well.

She continued blithely, 'Her blonde companion is Kate Lancaster, an old schoolfriend. She's also one of the highest paid models working in the US—originally from London via Dublin.'

Romain kept his expression bland with little effort. Years of controlling his emotions, of never allowing anyone to see inside his head came like second nature and dictated his actions. Affecting acute boredom, he ran his eyes over the friend.

The blonde was indeed exquisite—stunning. A sensual invitation of honeyed, lissome beauty. And... Nothing. No reaction. He had to remind himself his goal wasn't to pursue personal pleasure tonight. Even if catching his first sight of Sorcha Murphy had driven that thought from his mind and body.

He flicked his eyes back to Sorcha and felt his entire insides jolt...again...as though given an electric shock. He shrugged negligently, his hooded eyes hiding his reaction.

His aunt, apparently unaware of his efforts to appear blasé, saw his gaze resting on her. 'So...does she live up to her portfolio?'

'Of course. I wouldn't expect anything less from one of your models, Maud.'

He could feel his aunt preen beside him. She was nothing if not the best in the business for a reason.

'The question remains, however,' he drawled lightly, 'if she's got what it takes for a gruelling campaign, and whether she has in fact reformed from her wild ways...' He could sense his aunt bristle, and looked down into her flashing eyes. If he cast aspersions on one of her girls, then he cast aspersions on her.

'Romain, I won't tell you again. That was a long time ago. Not everyone is like your—'

'Maud…' he said warningly, with more than a hint of steel in his tone this time.

His aunt pursed her lips before saying, somewhat more tentatively, 'I assure you that I've never had a day's trouble with her. She's polite, punctual. Photographers and stylists love her.'

'You forget that I was working in the City in London eight years ago, when the tabloids were full of Sorcha Quinn, *enfant terrible*… The pictures and headlines are easy to conjure up again. It's not so long ago, and this campaign…well, it's sensitive.'

His aunt was beginning to sound exasperated. He knew she'd be coming to the end of her patience any minute now.

'And as I recall you didn't hold back your opinion then either, Romain. If she's survived to be here today under consideration for this job then you at least owe her a fair chance. It's not as if she came out of all that unscathed. It's why she changed her name to *Murphy*—which is how you didn't recognise her straight away when your board suggested her.'

The uncomfortable prickling assailed him again. He *hadn't* recognised her. In fact something in her pictures had reached out and touched him. In a place he'd prefer not to look. Thankfully his aunt was still talking, and it was easy to divert his thoughts.

'That's all behind her, Romain. I have a reputation to maintain too, believe me, and if there'd ever been a hint of trouble she'd have been out. I wouldn't have her on my books otherwise.'

Romain snorted discreetly. No leopard changed its spots so completely. He didn't doubt that quite a few of his aunt's models lived in such a way that if they were ever found out they'd be off the Models Inc register so fast their heads would spin. No. Women like Sorcha Murphy would keep their dirty little habits a secret. And if there was one thing he was fanatical about, it was that he never went near women involved with drugs. Professionally or socially. The very thought made his chest constrict with dark memories.

'I know you, Romain,' his aunt continued, sounding more confident. 'If you were seriously concerned about Sorcha Murphy's reputation you wouldn't have even considered her for this. Your board of directors obviously have no qualms about her past…'

His aunt had a point. And she didn't know that it was largely Sorcha's past and *apparent* redemption that had made them so keen to use her. For him, things weren't so straightforward.He stared across the room, finding it hard to tear his gaze away. Something was keeping him looking. Just as it had with her pictures. Some hint of vulnerability? A quality that many models failed abysmally to recreate for the camera. How could someone who looked so pure, so innocent, have been or—as was most likely—still *be* caught up in such a murky, corrupt world?

Just as he was thinking this, and feeling a surprising feeling of disappointment rushing through his veins, Sorcha Murphy looked across the room, almost as if she could sense the weight of his penetrating gaze. Their eyes locked. Blue and grey. And the world stopped turning.

Sorcha felt as though she'd just received a punch to her gut. And the only coherent thought she had in her head was: *How did I not notice him before?* There was a niggle of recognition, but she couldn't place him immediately, and the intensity in his eyes was making it hard to focus…

As though incapable of autonomous movement, her eyes could not move from the stranger's gaze. The most unusual steely grey, his eyes were cold…full of something…and she couldn't quite figure what it was. One thing it wasn't was *friendly*. She shivered inwardly, and yet still could not look away. Even though it was his eyes that held her as if ensnared in a web, she was also aware of his phenomenally dark good looks, the way he stood head and shoulders above anyone else, making him stand out in the crowd. Kate was forgotten. Everything was forgotten. Everything was distilled to this one moment and the tall dark man with the mesmerising eyes who kept staring, and staring. As bold as brass.

And then, in a split second of clarity, she read what was in his eyes. Condemnation and judgment.

A kind of disdain. Blatantly obvious. A look that had once been all too familiar in most people's eyes—one she hadn't seen for a long time. A tremble started somewhere in her legs, turning them to jelly, and panic seized her insides. Aghast at the strength of her reaction, with a few strangled muttered words she thrust her glass into Kate's free hand and walked through the crowd and out of the room, not even sure what she was running from.

'What on earth happened to you? One minute you were here, and the next you went as white as a ghost and stormed out of the room…'

Sorcha took her glass back from her friend and took a rare big gulp. She'd been in the toilets for the last ten minutes, holding a damp cloth to her skin in an effort to halt the rising tide of a nervous rash that hadn't appeared in years. She was still so stunned and shocked at her reaction to a mere look from that man across the room that she felt shaky. And in no mood to have her far too perceptive friend speculate on the possible reasons why.

One thing was for sure: with that blistering look she'd been transported back to another time. A time she did *not* want to remember. But he'd been with Maud. Surely they wouldn't have been talking about *her*? She hated the irrational feeling of unease it had given her. It had felt as though he'd been able to see right into the very soul of her…

'Nothing, Katie. I just had to go to the loo…'

'For ten minutes?' Katie snorted. 'I know you, Sorcha, and—'

Her friend broke off, seeing something behind Sorcha, over her shoulder, and then her hand was gripped so tight that she gasped. 'Katie!'

'Don't look now, but the most divine man is across the room…he's talking to Maud. He must be this nephew she said was coming tonight.' A look of comic disbelief made Kate's jaw drop. '*My God!* I've just realised who he is. But of course his pictures don't even do him justice… He's looking over here—'

'Katie…' Sorcha groaned, hiding her rising panic. It had to be him—the man she had seen across the room.

When Kate said her next words, they didn't even sink into Sorcha's head straight away because they were said with such breathy awe.

'*He's* Romain de Valois. Maud's nephew is Romain de Valois. It all makes sense now. The girls were talking about him backstage earlier. He's heading up some huge campaign—not to mention he's even *here*, and easily the most handsome man in New York… Of course they all think they're in with a—'

'*Romain de Valois?*' A horrified gasp made its way out of Sorcha's throat, which seemed to be tightening up. She'd gone horribly pale. Kate was oblivious.

'Yes…you must have heard of him. Oh, Sorcha, just *look*. He is seriously the most gorgeous specimen—'

'Katie.' Sorcha's voice was urgent, panicked. 'Don't you remember who he is?'

It seemed as though the fates were conspiring to throw her back down memory lane tonight whether she liked it or not.

Her mouth twisted into a bitter line. 'Please tell me you haven't forgotten that piece in the paper…the one that was worse than all the rest of them—the one that caused every other paper, every magazine and every photographer in London to turn their backs on me?'

Kate finally tore her gaze away from the man across the room and looked at Sorcha. Her brow creased for a second, and then her face became horrorstruck—about as horror struck as Sorcha felt.

Kate clutched her hand. 'Oh, God, Sorch…that was *him*. He gave that interview.'

Sorcha just nodded dumbly. Her insides seemed to be shrivelling up. Even eight years ago Romain de Valois had wielded enough influence to crush a fledgling career. He'd made her the black sheep among models. In a scathing interview he had denounced the use of drugs within the fashion world and had held her up as an example. Enough people had been terrified of losing his favour to seriously damage her reputation. Yet her naïve mistake had been far outweighed by the public scandal and the fallout. She'd been cruelly judged and tried for a crime she hadn't committed, and no one had been prepared to hear her side of the story. His power had been too great. And who cared about a skinny teenager? Within weeks there was already a new fresh face. A new lamb to the slaughter.

She'd been well aware of his name over the years, as he'd taken more and more control of the fashion industry and been mentioned more often with the kind of breathy awe that Kate had just shown. But Sorcha had always avoided listening in to conversations about him—had avoided reading about him, looking at pictures. It was a primal reflex to avoid anything that might make her remember that time in her life…and so far, despite his being Maud's nephew, as he was based primarily in Europe their paths hadn't crossed…

It was only the fact that she'd been able to go home to Ireland and start all over again that had saved her. Slowly but surely, with grit and determination, she'd built herself up again. She'd even taken her grandmother's maiden surname in an effort to start over, and so far, apart from a few snide comments, she'd managed to build a successful career. At least until today. Even though Maud knew of her past, and with characteristic aplomb had declared that it didn't matter to her, what mattered was how she behaved *now*, how could Sorcha fight against the poison she'd no doubt hear from her own nephew? Because that was surely what the topic of conversation had been, why he'd been looking at her like that…

'I'm so sorry, hon. I didn't remember…'

Sorcha squeezed Kate's hand. She knew her palm was clammy. 'Don't be silly. How were we to know *he'd* be the nephew Maud was going on about.'

Sorcha laughed, and it sounded a little hysterical to her ears. 'After all, she does have about a hundred of them, she's been married so many times. And Romain de Valois wouldn't even remember me, I'm sure.'

Kate smiled weakly, but Sorcha couldn't fail to notice how her gaze gravitated yet again over her shoulder to that man. She looked back to Sorcha almost guiltily. 'Look, it's not as if we have to talk to him or anything…'

Sorcha felt a curious compulsion unlike anything she'd ever felt before, and obeyed some rogue impulse to turn and look, to see again the man who had so carelessly judged her along with everyone else all those years ago. She felt herself turning… only to come eyeball to eyeball with that suddenly familiar light grey gaze across the room—a room that seemed to have shrunk in seconds. And he was now positively glowering at her!

Feeling every part of her rebel at the movement, Sorcha tore her eyes away again and looked back to Kate, who was watching her. Her friend whistled softly, arching one delicate blonde brow. She had missed nothing in the intense look.

'You spotted him before, didn't you? You didn't recognise him, but you shared a look just like *that*…and that's why you ran…'

Kate's words hit far too close to home and made Sorcha's voice uncustomarily sharp—a knee-jerk defence reaction to the riot of feelings and emotions swirling in her breast. 'Katie, I'll tell you right now exactly the sort of person he is. He's a holier-than-thou control freak. A wealthy, empty-headed playboy who turns up at the office only when he's not cavorting on some yacht somewhere, overloaded with silly dim-witted models who don't know their own names. He's lucky we've never crossed paths before, as quite frankly I've matured enough *not* to go over there and land him one, or throw my drink in his face for being such a pompous, bigoted—'

'Well, what's stopping you now…?'

Sorcha stopped dead. It was only then that she registered Kate's stunned look, her mouth gaping open inelegantly on an unspoken warning.

The low-pitched, dangerously accented deep voice came from so close behind her that she fancied she felt a hint of warm breath on her back. *Too late*. She hadn't even noticed. And now he was here, right behind her. And he had obviously heard every word which seemed to hang suspended accusingly in the air.

CHAPTER TWO

AS ROMAIN spoke he felt righteous anger move through him at her insulting words. But he also felt uncharacteristically at a loss. What on earth had possessed him to cross the room so soon? He couldn't even remember forming the wish or the desire to come closer…and yet here he was.

Her back faced him, her skin so pale that he doubted she'd ever been in the sun. And it was very lightly freckled. A true Celt.

It made her even more intriguing, added to her allure. An almost blue-black sheen rippled off her hair as she started to turn around, and when she faced him he sucked in a breath. She was, quite simply, ravishing. Almond-shaped blue eyes ringed with indecently long black lashes. Cheekbones so high and well defined that it was a sin that she wasn't smiling, to make her cheeks full and ripe. And her mouth… Lord, it must have been created by a god of decadence. The lush lower lip was a sensual invitation to touch, feel, slide his tongue across, and on it rested a top lip that was endearing with its slight overbite—

an exquisite anomaly in a perfect face, a cupid's bow of tempting irregularity.

Her breathing was rapid, her widening eyes overbright, the pupils dilated, and her skin flushed under his look. Something hard settled in his chest. He'd been right. He fought a silent battle with himself. Hadn't he just witnessed her little ten-minute trip to the powder room? Where he knew damn well that she and plenty of others like her would have been indulging in snorting a mood-enhancer…the most common kind on this circuit. She hadn't reformed.

He wanted to walk away, wanted to turn around and forget he'd ever seen her. But he also—perversely—never, ever wanted to let her out of his sight again. And he hated himself for it. And he hated *her* for attracting him so effortlessly. Yet he knew he was being irrational. And that fired him up even more.

'Yes…?'

Somehow she managed to articulate a word that sounded English, that made sense. Because one thing Sorcha knew for sure was nothing else made sense any more. Every preconceived notion about this man had fled. He was just a man, a devastatingly attractive man, holding her in some kind of wickedly sensual spell.

Tall, dark and handsome. He was a walking cliché. But no banal description could do justice to the way his hair shone almost black under the glittering lights. The way his hooded eyes hinted at a dangerous sensuality that was so palpable she felt faint. The way his skin shone and glowed with undeniable rude good health, so darkly olive that she fancied he must surely come from the Far East, despite being French. She was tall—almost five foot eleven—but she had to tip her face up to his. She was barely grazing his shoulder in heels.

The bespoke designer suit did little to hide the raw untamed sexuality of the man. Sorcha, from her experience of working with some of the best bodies in the business, knew a good physique when she saw it. His was…perfect. And she'd bet money that it wasn't honed in a gym. This man gave off an air of restless energy that spoke to her, called out to her. As a lover of the outdoors herself, she knew that he would only be content with pushing himself to the max, in the rawest of environments.

What had happened to her? Why couldn't she seem to move? She was vaguely aware that Kate had melted away seconds ago. And he was still looking at her as though he wanted to throttle her! For long moments they stared at each other in silent and heated communication. Finally Sorcha spoke again, more impatiently this time. Who did he think he was to come over and glower at her? She refused to give him the satisfaction of recognition.

'Yes? Can I help you?'

Romain had to focus. Her voice was husky, the accent refreshingly unjarring…melodious…. Clarity rushed back with force when a hapless waiter dropped a glass nearby, shocking him out of his stupor, making her flinch. And then he remembered. And that hardness took hold again.

Say hello, exchange a few words and get out of there—after all, hadn't he come here tonight to meet her? He might have decided to dismiss the notion of using her for the job, but a few words couldn't hurt…

He held out a hand. 'Romain de Valois. I don't believe we've actually met before…despite that flawless character reference.'

Finally some life force returned. She ignored his hand and said, with sweet acidity, 'Nearly as flawless as the one you gave me eight years ago?'

He dropped his hand and looked down at her, cool and unperturbed by her rudeness. 'So you do remember? I wasn't sure if your acerbic comments just now were due to intense dislike on first sight, or if you were referring to that.'

She couldn't hide the bitterness. 'Of course I remember, Monsieur de Valois. It's not every day the press chases a seventeen-year-old out of London, calling for her blood—a press that was spurred on by *your* comments. All you lacked was a pulpit…' Her chest rose and fell and she couldn't disguise her agitation. She could feel her skin heating up under his look.

'Do you forget that you were a seventeen-year-old drug addict?' he said with harsh inflection. 'Photographed unconscious on the street?'

A pain so sharp that it caused her to stop breathing for a second made Sorcha want to curl inwards.

Guilt, shame, and an old, old fear all vied for supremacy. With what felt like a superhuman effort she found some hard brittle shell left. She tossed her hair with studied indifference, and was too wound up to notice the tiny flash in the cool grey gaze.

Her voice was scathing. 'If you've got nothing more to do than come over here like some kind of outdated moral judge and check for track marks on my arms, then please excuse me—' She turned to go, and was taking a step away when her wrist was caught in a strong grip. His touch seared through her whole body like a brand. He slowly and very calmly turned her palm upwards, and made a thorough study up and down the underside of her milky white arm.

'No,' he said musingly. 'No track marks. But then I'm sure you're an intelligent woman. You'd have them well hidden.'

Sorcha finally yanked her arm free and hugged it close to her chest, as though he had burnt her. Her voice was shaking with emotion, and to her utter horror she could feel the sting of tears at the back of her eyelids. 'Mr de Valois, if you would please excuse me? I am here in a work capacity tonight for your aunt. I don't want to cause a scene, but trust me when I say that if you try to stop me leaving again I will scream this room down.'

'There's no need for such dramatics Miss Murphy—or should I say *Quinn*? And if you did anything of the sort I'd put you over my shoulder and carry you out like a child having a tantrum.'

Sorcha gulped, her bravado in short supply all of a sudden. She didn't doubt his words for a second, and the thought of him throwing her over his impossibly broad shoulder… She could feel the heat flare up from her stomach.

She furiously willed a body which seemed to have been invaded by an alien force to obey her silent command to stop reacting to his presence, and gritted out, 'It's Murphy to you. If all you want is to see the tabloid fodder you chewed up and spat out, then have a good look.'

'Oh, I am,' he drawled, and Sorcha mentally castigated herself for her careless words.

She didn't want this man's attention on her…*any part of her*.

'You've certainly grown up…and filled out.'

She sucked in a breath, unaware that her innocent movement caused his eyes to be drawn back to those parts of her body where they had rested briefly in an eloquent accompaniment to his words.

'I was just a teenager—'

'No teenager I knew stayed out till six a.m. every morning, drinking champagne all night, taking cocktails of various drugs to stay awake—'

He glanced pointedly at the glass in her hand. Her knuckles were white on the stem because she gripped it so tightly. Following his glance, and feeling suddenly reckless and rebellious, she tipped the glass to him in a salute. 'Well, I must say it's nice to meet the man who once called me the poison seeping into the industry… Here's to you, Mr de Valois. I wish you luck on your crusade to rid the world of imperfect people!'

And with that Sorcha downed the half empty glass in one go. Very carefully she put it down on a nearby table. And while she still could, feeling sick from the immediate rush of a drink she didn't usually favour, she spun on impossibly high heels and strode away from him, the silk of her long dress billowing out behind her.

More than a few men turned to look as she passed, and Romain couldn't fail to notice, the very strange and proprietorial surge of…something very disturbing. He felt a little shell shocked. He could still see the white expanse of her delicate throat, bared as she had downed the sparkling drink. Her eyes had flashed before putting the glass down.

No woman had *ever* walked away from him like that, or showed such blatant disrespect. Yet, much to his utter confusion, he found himself thinking that his decision to veto her for the campaign suddenly seemed a little too hasty. Watching her walk away had filled him with the almost overwhelming urge to grab her back, strike more sparks, keep her talking.

He hadn't expected this. He'd expected her to be hard, with that smooth shell most models had, yet her vulnerability had hit him straight between the eyes. And he'd been surprised that she'd remembered his comments from eight years previously. His jaw hardened. Despite his aunt's words, and Sorcha

Murphy's *apparent* vulnerability, he'd be more than surprised to find that she had given up her old habits.

To be brutally honest, he'd expected that once she'd known who he was she'd morph into exactly the type of woman he'd become immune to. Sycophantic, posturing… But she hadn't. She'd been filled with fire and passion underneath that pale, pale skin. An intoxicating package.

For some men, he told himself angrily, and finally turned away from the image of her slender back walking away from him.

'Well, he can take his job and—'

'Sorcha!' Maud's husky smoke-ravaged voice rang out like the crack of a whip.

It stopped Sorcha in her tracks—literally. She was pacing back and forth in Maud's palatial office that looked out over busy New York streets. Ever since Maud had called her in to tell her that Romain de Valois wanted *her* for his campaign, she'd been feeling jittery and panicky.

She sat down. 'Sorry, Maud, I know he's your nephew—'

'Technically, he's my ex-nephew.' The older woman waved a hand. 'That doesn't matter anyway. Nepotism didn't get him where he is now; that was through sheer hard graft and ingenuity.' Her face softened with unmistakable affection. 'Can you believe even *I* have to answer to him?' She ignored Sorcha's dark scowl, austerity marking her features again. 'The fact is, this is probably one of the most prestigious jobs you could ever be offered—two weeks jet-setting around the world. Do you know how many models were considered? It's so important to him that he's overseeing the whole shoot personally. He's even willing to kick off in Ireland to accommodate your holiday plans—a condition *I* insisted on.'

The thought of even a day with that man glowering down his nose at her, checking up on her every two minutes, caused very contradictory feelings in Sorcha's head…and body. Since that night almost a week ago she hadn't been able to get his dark face and tall, impressive body out of her mind. And she hated it. He was her nemesis—the embodiment of every misunderstanding she had suffered all those years ago.

'Maud…can't you see how difficult this would be? He's not just anyone. He's—'

'I'm well aware of the things he said in London that time. But you have to admit, innocent or not, if you hadn't been caught like that then he wouldn't have had any reason to say anything. His hand was forced by his board. He didn't have the complete control he enjoys now. They couldn't be seen to be taking an easy line on models doing drugs…not when that girl had died so soon before…'

Sorcha felt cold all of a sudden. She was barely able to take in Maud's words, her mind seizing on the girl that she'd mentioned. She had been a young model on the brink of stardom who'd overdosed and died only weeks before Sorcha's own chain of events had unfolded. It always made her feel sick, and impotent with anger and guilt. It was one of the reasons she'd finally followed her heart in the past year and tried to do something about those past events—something concrete…

Maud stood up and came round to perch one hip on her desk. She looked at Sorcha from over her spectacles. 'I'll tell you something else that no one knows…' She sighed. 'It might help you understand…'

Sorcha looked at Maud curiously.

'His own mother was a drug addict. She died of an overdose. So, you see, he has a very personal abhorrence of drugs.'

Sorcha felt a dart of sympathy. But then she remembered the condemnation in his eyes and forced her mind to clear the images she always worked so hard to avoid. She said, somewhat stiltedly, 'Well, his own personal issues aside, I'm sorry for him— but that doesn't excuse his behaviour. When he spoke to me the other night it was obvious he still believes that I'm involved in something. He's not willing to give me the benefit of the doubt. I'm sorry, Maud, but I'm taking my few months out. You know I've been promising this to myself for the past year.'

Her eyes beseeched her agency boss. Maud looked fierce for a second, and then shrugged. 'I think you're mad, Sorcha. I'll let him know, but I warn you—once he's decided on something he's not one to give up easily. He may even try to go through your Irish agency, knowing that you're headed back there. His board of management are adamant about using you...'

Sorcha shot to her feet. 'See! He's been forced into this against his will. He won't push it if I refuse. Please, just tell him and see for yourself. He'll walk away without a backward glance.'

Sorcha closed her eyes and gripped the handrest as the plane took off. She *hated* take-offs. She always imagined the bottom of the plane scraping along the ground at the last moment, and then there was that wobbly bit as it fought for equilibrium in the air—

'Are you all right, dear?'

She opened her eyes and looked at the kind, elderly woman on her right. She smiled weakly, but she could feel the sweat on her brow and knew she must be pale from the concerned look the woman was giving her.

'Fine. Sorry—I just hate taking off. No matter how often I fly, it doesn't get better.'

'Ah, well, sure it's only a short enough flight. We'll be home in no time.'

Sorcha smiled and turned back to look out of the window. *Home*. Ireland. She'd only been back intermittently between jobs in the past year, to work on her project whenever she had the chance, and she'd missed it—missed her apartment. The home she shared with Kate in New York was Kate's. But her place in Dublin was *hers*. Bought and paid for with her own hard-earned money.

The plane was stabilising at last, so Sorcha's hands eased their death grip and she sat back and closed her eyes. It had been ten days since the night of the function in New York, and she hadn't stopped working since then. Every day had been packed to the brim. Even so *that* man—his voice, his face, his air of intense, focused energy—would slip into her consciousness and take up residence.

Just thinking about him made her heart speed up, her breath quicken. And made a whole host of other sensations race through her body. She hated that she could be having this kind of reaction to someone who had so carelessly played God with her life, her career. She forced herself to relax. Hadn't she walked away from him? Yet the look in his eyes when she'd left him standing there that night had been so intense… Maud hadn't had to warn her. She was *sure* that he was a man who would be single-minded in his pursuit of anything… or anyone.

Since leaving Maud's office, only three days before, she'd half expected him to turn up at any moment and demand that she do the job—which she couldn't believe she'd even been considered for, if it was half as amazing as Maud had outlined. There were plenty more models who were far more ambitious, who always got the big campaigns. So why had not seeing him, not hearing anything, led her to feel like a cat on a hot tin roof? Why had she found herself jumping every time the phone rang, only to be in some tiny and very treacherous way *disappointed* when it had just been Katie or her brother?

She'd met the man for mere moments, and he had proved himself to be every bit as arrogant, judgmental and overbearing as she would have expected. Why did it have to be someone like *him* who seemed to be cracking through the armour she'd erected around herself for so long? Why couldn't someone else be making her heart quicken, her breath shorten just thinking of them? Someone nice, unassuming, non-threatening. Someone who would be gentle, kind, sensitive. Certainly not tall, powerful, dark and mysterious…arrogant, overbearing, too confident, too sexual—

'So, dear, were you on holiday in America?'

Sorcha nearly jumped out of her skin—she'd been so intent on listing Romain de Valois's negative attributes to herself.

She shook her head, as much to herself as anyone else, and smiled.

'No…unfortunately not. I've been working…'

With some kind of cowardly relief, she allowed herself to be sucked into inane conversation. Anything to stop dangerous thoughts and images circulating in her head. It wasn't as if she was ever going to meet him again anyway…

Sorcha's mobile was ringing as soon as she arrived at her apartment. She dumped her suitcase and fished it out of her handbag. No number was listed on the

screen, but she figured it was because it was either
Katie, her mother or her over-protective big brother,
checking in to see if she'd landed in one piece, and
they were all abroad. She smiled as she answered.

'OK, whichever one of you it is. I'm fine, I've just
landed, and the plane didn't crash—although at one
stage I seriously thought—'

'Hello, Sorcha.'

Words froze on her lips. Her mouth stayed open.
Her throat dried. That voice. His voice. Deep, au-
thoritative, sensual. Disturbingly close. Her hand
gripped the phone tight.

'I'm sorry, who is this?'

A soft chuckle made her insides quiver. 'You're
pretending to have forgotten me already?'

The conceited arrogance of the man! She knew
very well who it was, and hated that he could be *here*,
in her space, even if just on the end of a tenuous connection. She felt guilty—as though she'd conjured
him up with her imaginings. She would not give him
the satisfaction of letting him know that she knew it
was him. Even though she burned to know what he
wanted.

As if reading her every thought, he spoke with
low, seductive deadliness. 'I got your number from
Maud, who informed me of your plans to go home.
I know you've probably just arrived, but I wanted to
get in touch with you as soon as possible.'

Sorcha closed her eyes for a second, knowing it
would be futile to pretend ignorance of the power he

had. The man was so confidently arrogant that he hadn't even given her time to play dumb.

'Yes, I am back in Dublin now. Thousands of miles from New York. I'm taking a well-earned break—'

'I've got a job proposal to discuss with you.'

Sorcha's mouth opened and closed, a whole host of conflicting emotions see—sawing through her at the realisation that he *was* determined to pursue her for this job. But it would be untenable, unthinkable—surely he could see that?

'I'm afraid I'm not doing any jobs for the foreseeable future. I've been working back to back for the past year—not that it's any business of yours—and now I'm taking time off. As I told Maud before I left, I'm sure you'll find another model who can do whatever it is you have in mind. Thanks for the call, though. Goodbye.'

She was in the act of taking the phone away from her ear, about to switch it off, when she heard a silky,

'*Wait.* You might want to hear what I have to say about the job.'

Reluctantly she brought the phone back to her ear. 'I've already explained—'

'I'm here in Dublin too, actually. I arrived yesterday. Charming city.'

Sorcha nearly dropped the phone in shock, her hand suddenly sweaty. *He was here? In Dublin?*

Feeling very agitated, she walked over to her fourth-floor window and looked down to the street outside—almost as if he might be standing there looking up at her. But the road surrounding her side of Merrion Square was empty, the inner-city rush hour traffic having been and gone. Her heart was pumping erratically.

Trying not to sound panicked, she said lightly, 'That's great. Enjoy your visit, Monsieur de Valois. There are plenty of very good modelling agencies—'

'I had a lovely meeting this afternoon with your Irish agent Lisa. Very accommodating. I've given her the brief for the job, and she agrees with me that you're perfect for what we're looking for.'

Sorcha closed her eyes again and sank into the couch just behind her, under the window. This was exactly what Maud had warned her he might do. It was what she'd been hoping to avoid—at least until she'd booked herself some secluded time away. She hadn't told her Irish agent that she was coming home, knowing full well that she'd have her booked to within an inch of her life before she'd even stepped off the plane. Sorcha was one of their biggest success stories and exports, and Lisa was the agent who had spotted her in the first place. She always felt duty-bound to do as much work for her as she could whenever she came home…as some sort of payback for having defected to the States.

'So, Lisa knows I'm home…' she said dully—as if she even needed to ask.

'She does.'

He sounded so smug that Sorcha sat forward on her

couch, anger surging through her veins at the thought that this man, in his stubborn pursuit of whatever it was he wanted, had scuppered her plans for rest and relaxation—not to mention the time she'd put aside to work on the important project that was so dear to her heart. 'Why are you doing this? You can't seriously mean to work with me. You've made your opinion abundantly clear, Monsieur de Valois, and I won't have you watching my every move. Just because you can't handle someone turning you down—'

'Careful, Sorcha.' His voice for the first time sounded hard and lethal.

She stopped despite herself.

'All I'm suggesting is that you meet with Lisa tomorrow. She will tell you what I'm proposing. The decision as to whether or not you want to meet me to discuss the job further will be entirely up to you. No one will force you to do this.'

CHAPTER THREE

NO-ONE *will force you to do this...*

They wouldn't have to, Sorcha thought grimly as she walked the short journey from her agent's office to Romain's exclusive hotel the following day. Lisa had told her where he'd be for their '*meeting*'. She had to hand it to him. He must have walked into the small Irish modelling agency and laughed out loud. It would have been like taking candy from a baby.

She could picture it now: the industry's most powerful head—a person who held the kind of authority that would make anyone dizzy, a man responsible for countless designers and their merchandise and advertising, not to mention his high profile as one of the world's most eligible and handsome men— walked into a tiny basement agency, offered them a deal for one of their models that was in excess of six figures... Well, you wouldn't have to be a rocket scientist to do the maths.

When Sorcha had walked in that morning the place had been buzzing, the excitement palpable. Pretty Woman was not one of the most successful agencies in Dublin, but it was friendly, the girls were lovely, and Lisa had become a good friend to Sorcha. When her career had started to take off in Dublin, and then London, Sorcha had refused to leave Lisa's representation, despite being told it could sabotage her career. And then when the tide had turned against her Lisa had remained loyal in the face of scathing public opinion. Her debt to Lisa was much the same as her one to Katie. Never mentioned, never referred to, but *there*.

Sorcha was well aware that Pretty Woman wasn't doing as well as other agencies. In fact the last time she'd been home Lisa had confided to her that if not for Sorcha the agency might have to close down. So now what was she supposed to do? Romain de Valois had just offered them a massively lucrative job—Lisa had even mentioned that they were hoping to expand their offices on the back of it! The proviso, of course, was that Sorcha had to be the model. Romain had told Lisa that he would not under any circumstances even entertain looking at anyone else.

Seething silently, she made her way through the pedestrian crush on the streets. The air was mild, and blue skies made Dublin look its best, but she barely noticed. Romain de Valois had painted her into a corner and thrown away the brush.

She crossed a busy road and the huge hotel loomed magnificent and ornate just opposite, gleaming in the sunshine. It stood overlooking the main city park, which bloomed with colour. Everything fled her mind as she approached closer and closer. And again she remonstrated with herself. How could such a brief meeting in one night have made such an impact? Why had he pushed her buttons so easily? She didn't want to know, she told herself hastily. And now he was here…controlling her life like a puppet master.

She let the indignation rise. Anything to help block out the far more conflicting feelings—like one in particular, which felt suspiciously and awfully like excitement at the thought of seeing him again.

Romain sat in a high-backed chair at the rear of the main reception room in the recently refurbished Shelbourne Hotel. With his elbows on the armrests, he rested his chin on steepled fingers. He'd positioned himself in such a way that he would see Sorcha arrive before she saw him.

A necessary precaution, as he was suddenly questioning his very sanity. After that night something compelling had taken him over. When further pushed by Maud, who'd assured him of Sorcha's professionalism *again*, and then by his board it had seemed almost easy to give in, to allow himself to be swayed. And now he couldn't remember the last time, if ever, he'd flown halfway across the world to chase a woman. His mouth compressed. He might try to dress it up, call it something else, pretend to himself that his main motive was to get her for this very genuine ad campaign—which he still couldn't believe she'd had the temerity to turn down—but the reality, as he knew well, was that she was the first woman who'd walked away from him.

His mouth twisted. Yet if he could make sure that she behaved, make sure she stayed clean, then perhaps…this could work. After all, he would be on hand every step of the way to ensure things went the way he wanted. He didn't usually consider mixing business with pleasure, but now…He was at a stage in his career where his absolute control meant he could do as he pleased…he was beholden to none. Maybe for once he could relax that rigid control a little. The thought of taming Sorcha Murphy was making that sense of dissatisfaction a distant memory.

And then in an instant she was *there*. That jolt went through his body again, taking him by surprise. His eyes ran over her hungrily, as if inspecting a thoroughbred. From the tip of her shiny black hair, tied back into a low ponytail, to the plain white shirt and casual jacket over worn jeans, all the way to the scuffed runners on her feet. She'd made no effort to impress him—the staid black frames of the sensible glasses perched on her nose said that—and yet her beauty was ethereal and intoxicatingly earthy, just as he had remembered. Unlike other models, who sometimes looked strange in real life, their proportions working for the camera but weirdly not in the flesh, Sorcha looked as good off the page, if not even better, and that was rare. A frisson of excitement ran through him as he saw the concierge point in his direction and their eyes met.

Let the battle commence.

* * *

As Sorcha approached Romain, she felt as self conscious as she had her first day on a catwalk. She had that same unsettling reaction she'd had in New York. All of her antipathy, all of her preconceived notions fled as she walked towards him—and then he compounded it by standing with lithe grace. Even taller, broader, more powerful than she remembered. Darker… That hint of Far Eastern lineage struck her again. She reached him, he held out a hand. This time, still in shock to think that he could be *here*, Sorcha let her hand be taken by his. It was firm, cool. His fingers closed around hers and she felt a crazy pulse throb fleetingly and disturbingly between her legs.

'Sorcha.' He indicated a seat opposite and didn't let go of her hand until she sat down. When she finally got it back it was tingling.

She wished for some sanity for reality to come back into her head, which felt woozy. She was determined not to be staying for longer than a few minutes at the most, and perched uncomfortably on the edge of her chair. All previous thoughts of Pretty Woman and Lisa fled in proximity to this man.

'Mr de Valois—'

'I didn't know you wore glasses.'

Sorcha's mouth stayed open. She felt nonplussed until she put up a hand and felt the familiar frames on her nose. She'd been so preoccupied that she hadn't even noticed that she'd forgotten to take them off.

Even though her eyes weren't so bad that she needed them right now, she suddenly wanted to keep them on.

'Well, I'm sorry if they're putting you off, Mr de Valois. I'm afraid, along with my other failings, I'm also slightly long-sighted.'

He tutted and lifted a hand to call for service, before fixing her with that steely gaze again. 'Not at all. They suit you. And please don't put yourself down—'

'Why? Because you'll do that for me?'

For a second there was no reaction, and then a huge smile lit his harshly handsome face, making him look years younger and so gorgeous that Sorcha felt welded to her chair. Wasn't she supposed to be walking out by now? He looked ridiculously exotic against the backdrop of the opulent Dublin hotel, surrounded by the more pale, Celtic-skinned customers. His accent was pronounced, heightening that sense of his otherness in this place.

'As sparky as I remember…that's good.'

Sorcha felt like grinding her teeth. 'I'm not trying to be sparky, Mr de Valois. I'm here to tell you that I'm not interested in your job.'

He waved a dismissive hand. 'Let's order some tea, yes? I believe it is something of a national delicacy…and then we will have lunch.'

'You're not listening to me, Mr de Valois—'

'No,' he said with silken deadliness. 'You are not listening to me. And please call me Romain—after all, we will be working closely together for the next few weeks, and I hate to stand on ceremony…'

Sorcha just looked at him and shook her head. The smooth conceit and downright arrogance of the man was unbelievable.

'*Mr* de Valois, unless you plan on tying me to this chair there is nothing to stop me standing up and walking out of here. I've told Maud and now you that I'm not interested in the job. I'm due to take some holiday—'

She had to stop when a waitress came and delivered the tea. Sorcha couldn't even remember the order having been taken. She watched, disgusted, at the way the pretty young blonde girl blushed a deep shade of crimson when Romain smiled at her and said thank you. The poor girl practically fell over a chair as she left, her eyes glued to what was probably the most stupendously handsome man she'd ever seen in her young life. Romain de Valois, of course, had already forgotten her, and was focusing those long-lashed grey eyes back on Sorcha, with an intensity that threatened to scramble her brains all over again.

Romain was glad of the short distraction of the waitress, because the shaft of pure arousal that had gone straight to his groin when Sorcha had mentioned being tied to the chair had thrown up other images…much more explicit…of her being tied to a bed… He fought to regain some composure, to remember what she had said.

'Which is why we are going to start the campaign here.' He held out a cup of tea, 'Tell me, did you also mention to Lisa that you were not going to take the job?'

The sickening knowledge of how neatly he'd manipulated events brought her some much needed focus back—even though she knew with a sinking feeling in her belly that it would be futile to keep insisting that she wouldn't do the job. She also had to accept the cup he was offering her, or risk causing a scene. She saw a glint of triumph light his eyes, as if he could read her thoughts. He was getting under her skin in a prickly heat kind of way that made her very nervous. It made her voice clipped, arctic. 'In light of past…events—namely your very public condemnation of me—' She stopped as she realised she'd been about to say *at a very painful time in my life*. She knew that she didn't want him to see that vulnerable side of her, so she faltered for a second, her skin heating up. 'I find it hard to see why you want me to do this campaign so badly.'

Romain studied her. She looked about ready to spring off the chair and bolt. And right at that moment all he wanted to do was get up, throw her over his shoulder and carry her upstairs to his suite, loosen her hair, take off her glasses, uncover her body inch by inch, see if those soft swells that he could just glimpse under her shirt were really as voluptuous as they looked… He sat back.

He was not a Neanderthal. He was sophisticated and urbane. This woman might be appealing to the most basic level of his carnal urges, but it was probably because he hadn't had a woman in a while and she was refreshingly different from the cool blondes he usually favoured. He sipped his tea and carefully placed the cup back onto the saucer.

'The fact is, I had decided that we could do without you on this campaign, and was prepared to tell my board so—'

'See?' The relief was evident in Sorcha's voice, in the way her face cleared, and she put down her cup and half rose from her chair. 'That's fine with me. Thanks for the tea—'

'Sit down.'

Sorcha responded to the very explicit threat in his voice, sitting down again before she'd even realised what she was doing. The memory of him threatening to throw her over his shoulder was all too recent. And, as unmistakably urbane as this man was, there was an air of danger about him, a disregard for convention, the niceties.

'But after seeing you in the flesh...'

When he said that his words were loaded with a sensual meaning that was not lost on her. Sorcha's head went so fuzzy for a second that she missed his next immediate words.

'You would be perfect for the job. The only suitable model, in fact.'

She shook her head, trying to clear it, and took her glasses off for a moment to pinch the bridge of her nose in an endearingly personal reflex, something she only ever did when under pressure or stressed.

'Monsieur de Valois—'

'Romain, please.' He smiled, and it was the smile of a shark.

Sorcha gave in. Perhaps this was the way to reach him. She put her glasses back on and said in her most businesslike voice, 'Very well—Romain.' She ignored the way saying his name made a funny flutter start in her chest. 'I'm sure your board can be persuaded to take on another model to fit their visual concepts. There has to be a million other women out there with my colouring.' She laughed and it sounded strained. 'I mean, all you have to do is step outside this hotel and you'll find hundreds.'

Romain's mouth quirked. She really had no idea how stunning she was. Was she fishing for compliments? But the look on her face was so earnest it made something in his chest tighten.

He shook his head brusquely. 'Not as many as you would think. And none with your unique…past.'

She bristled immediately. 'What's that got to do with anything?'

'It's inspired the whole concept of this campaign. This is no ordinary shoot, Sorcha. Only at its most basic level is it to be a showcase for numerous luxury goods, the season's finest offerings. With the way society is going—the fascination between people and media, the cult of celebrity…you represent someone who was torn down—'

'Thanks to you,' she said bitterly, picking up her cup again with a jerky movement. But Romain ignored her comment, continuing as if he hadn't heard her.

'…and built herself up again. You've shown a tenacity of spirit, if you will. A grit and determination to succeed at all costs. You represent redemption. You've weathered a storm and come out the other side. People nowadays won't buy the image of the virginal prom queen—they resonate more with a fallible person. I'm willing to give you the benefit of the doubt, take my board's and my aunt's word that you *are* reliable. But trust me, Sorcha, if there's a hint of any kind of scandal or drugs I won't hesitate to drop you, and you won't receive a penny. However, as long as I see no evidence of anything…' He spread his hands and shrugged eloquently.

His words made Sorcha reel slightly. She hadn't had her past raked up so comprehensively in years. Or reduced to such succinct devastation. The cup she held in her hand shook slightly, and she put it down with a clatter. She felt as if a layer of skin had been stripped off. 'Well, I'm delighted that someone has seen fit to take the scrap metal of my life and see it fashioned into something that can benefit the greater good of the advertising industry.'

Romain uncharacteristically felt at a loss for words—as if he had somehow made an error of judgment. Sorcha was expressionless. Cold and aloof. Without even knowing how, he *knew* that he'd hurt her—and that knowledge threw him. As it had when he'd seen that vulnerability up close. The hard sheen he'd expected to find hadn't been there. And the vulnerability was there again now—just under the surface.

With what felt uncomfortably like relief, he saw the head waiter from the restaurant approach. He stood and gestured with a hand. 'I've booked us a table for lunch. Why don't we continue this discussion over some food?'

It wasn't a question, and Sorcha felt too shell shocked to argue. Mute, she preceded him out of the reception room and into the restaurant, where gold-coloured banquette seats made their table into a gilded prison of privacy.

CHAPTER FOUR

ONCE seated, Sorcha avoided looking at the unnerving man opposite her. Out of the corner of her eye she could see long brown fingers curled around the edges of the menu, and her heart started to beat fast again. It was some moments before she realised that he was looking at her expectantly. Taking a deep breath, she closed her menu too, having no idea of what it offered.

'So...how long have you needed glasses?' He threw her with such an innocuous question after his last words, which had been so rawly personal. She looked at him warily and was glad of the table between them, and the sturdy frames of her glasses. Perversely, they seemed to give her some protection—as if projecting an image that made her more comfortable in such close proximity to his potent sexuality.

'Relatively recently. Years of late nights cramming for exams have taken their toll—I find I need them for reading, or if I'm tired.'

His brow quirked. 'A hangover from school?

Surely it's been some time since you crammed for anything?'

It wasn't really a question, but Sorcha wanted to blurt out defensively that the for the past four years she'd been studying late into the night almost every night. It was one of her most cherished accomplishments—and she'd been about to tell *him*. Her mouth was still open. Horror filled her at how close she'd come to telling him something so personal. The thought of his reaction if she had made her go cold.

She shut her mouth and smiled sweetly. 'Well, what do you expect? With all the partying I was doing I hardly had time to worry about the state of my eyes, now, did I?'

Her words struck a hollow chord in Romain somewhere. He looked at her intently, but she'd already picked up the menu again. Her whole frame was tight with tension. For a brief second there something so passionate had crossed her face that he'd fully expected her to say something else entirely...but *what*?

'You do seem to live quite the quiet life now, or are you just careful about where and when you're seen, having learnt from past experience?'

The tone in his voice made all sorts of implications about why she might want to hide or not be seen. He was lounging back, at perfect ease, his suit jacket gone, his shirt open at the throat, stretched across his formidable chest. Sorcha sat up straight. She'd let her guard down for one second too many, and the thought that he must have had her investigated in some way made her feel violated.

'If I do take on this job—which it would appear I have very little choice *but* to do—I will not be subjected to this kind of questioning. You know nothing about me or my past. *Nothing.* I will never tell you anything about my personal life.'

He inclined his head with a minute gesture, but Sorcha could see that she'd got to him. His eyes had flashed a stormy grey for a second.

He leant forward and said silkily, 'Never say never…'

She became aware that the waiter was hovering, and Romain, supremely cool again, looked up to indicate that they were ready to order. Sorcha had never felt so many conflicting emotions and sensations before. She very much wanted to run away— get away from this disturbing man whose mere presence seemed to have the power to reach inside her and shine a light on her innermost vulnerabilities.

Romain ordered the fish special, and Sorcha ordered a steak with mash. He reacted almost comically to her order. Sorcha caught his look and read it in a second. How could she forget that she was in the presence of a serial lothario? After that night in New York Katie had been only too eager to fill her in on his reputation, which would have made Casanova blush. Her mouth tightened. He was used to this, of course. Taking models out. Wining and dining them.

And no doubt he'd never heard any of them ask for anything more substantial than a lettuce leaf dressed with half a grape.

She caught the waiter just before he left the table and smiled broadly. 'Could you make that a double portion of mash, please?'

When she looked back to Romain she could see what looked suspiciously like a twitch on his mouth. Damn him. Her small childish gesture felt flat and silly now.

They sat looking at each other for a long moment. Sorcha refused to be the one to break her gaze first. And when he spoke she felt light-headed—as if she'd scored some tiny yet triumphant victory.

'Let me tell you a little more about the campaign. I feel that perhaps I didn't give you the full picture before.'

Sorcha's tone was a dry as sandpaper. 'Don't worry—I get the picture. You've got it in for me, and even though I'll be getting paid, it'll be Sorcha Murphy to the gallows again. Although this time with silk gloves on.'

He looked at her for a long moment and felt a surge of something rush through him. Her self deprecation caught him off guard. He wasn't used to women displaying that kind of humour around him. Not ones who looked like Sorcha Murphy.

'To an extent you might perceive that to be the case. And based on what I said earlier I can't blame you. However, it's not an entirely accurate picture…'

Sorcha was surprised to find that he was almost apologising, as if he knew he'd been less than sensitive. She found herself nodding slightly, as if to encourage him to continue, and knew that while she wished she could have walked away well before now, having told him what he could do with his job, another part of her was only too happy to be here, experiencing this man's full wattage up close.

At that moment, before he could continue, the waiter arrived at the table with a bottle of wine. Romain tasted it, and took the liberty of pouring them both a glass. Sorcha felt as though perhaps she shouldn't take any—as if drinking wine might somehow confirm his bad opinion of her—and then berated herself. She wasn't going to change anything for him. She didn't care about his opinion, she told herself staunchly.

He tipped his glass in a mocking salute, and Sorcha took a sip from hers. The cool crisp white wine slipped down her throat like velvet. She thought dimly that it had no right to taste, *feel* so good in such a situation.

His beautifully shaped brown hand played with his glass, distracting her. She felt like clamping a hand over his to stop him, felt annoyed with him for having this power...and then he spoke again, bringing her attention back to his face and his mouth, which was even worse.

'What I was talking about—using you for what you can bring to the campaign in terms of your past…your apparent redemption…quite apart from your undeniable beauty…'

Sorcha went pink. She hated it when anyone made reference like that to her looks. She quickly took a sip of her drink before he could notice. But he frowned slightly, those dark brows drawing together as if she puzzled him. She didn't want to puzzle him. She didn't want him to look any further than Sorcha Murphy the model, who would stand in front of a photographer and get the shots they required.

'Go on. Please.' Her voice sounded slightly strangled, and she breathed a sigh of relief when the intensity left his face.

'Your past would never be mentioned, never alluded to. What I'm talking about is a…subliminal message, if you will. Counting on the fact that people will see you and may remember, or not, where you came from, what happened…That will elevate the campaign beyond the ordinary, because they will empathise with you.'

'This must be some campaign if you're putting this much thought into it,' she said, somewhat shakily.

He nodded. 'It is very special. Like I said, it *is* to showcase a selection of luxury goods and clothes supplied by my various companies, but it's also going to promote a way of living. It's a move away from the vigorous advertising that is common now—this will be much more…dreamlike…evocative. It centres on two people—a man and a woman—who we follow as they travel all across the world in a romantic game of cat and mouse...'

Sorcha felt for a very uncanny moment as if he might be talking about *them*—but that was ridiculous.

Interested despite herself, she shrugged minutely. 'That does sound...intriguing.'

'And is it killing you to say that?' he asked with a mocking smile.

She shook her head, eyes flashing.

He sat forward then, making her nervous. 'Lisa also mentioned something else to me.'

Now Sorcha was really nervous. Her mind raced... Surely Lisa wouldn't have told him about—?

'The youth outreach centre?'

Sorcha blanched, and Romain saw her reaction. Her eyes were two huge pools of liquid blue, and that damned vulnerability was back.

Sorcha couldn't believe it. How could Lisa have done that? Although, after sitting with the man for less than an hour, Sorcha knew what a physical struggle it was to resist him.

'What did she tell you?' She asked tightly, every line of her body screaming with tension.

'Just that you've been working on it for the past few years, and it's due to open a couple of weeks after we finish shooting...'

Every ounce of self-protection in Sorcha rose up. This was so close to the heart of her, such a treasured secret, that even to be *discussing* it with him was overwhelming. And worse, if he decided to delve any deeper… Sorcha started to shake inwardly. 'Yes. It is. But it's no concern of yours—'

'Or yours either, apparently. Lisa said that you've only been back periodically to oversee the building in the past year.'

The unfairness of his attack made Sorcha reel slightly. She saw spots before her eyes. But she realised quickly that if he thought that, then she could in fact use it.

She lifted one slim shoulder and glanced away, but try as she might she couldn't totally disguise her turmoil. She looked back at Romain and steeled herself. 'Like I said, it's none of your business *what* my involvement is in the outreach centre…' She faltered. She felt as if she was jinxing it just talking about it with him. 'So I'd appreciate it if you don't bring it up again.'

He ignored her. 'Tell me, Sorcha, is it all part of the façade? To make people think you've changed? Did you see someone else, another celebrity, do something similar and think that you'd do the same?' Cynicism twisted his beautiful mouth. 'After all, you can't beat the publicity you'll get on the day. Tell me have you already picked out what you're going to wear as you cut the ribbon?'

Sorcha sat back. A wave of hurt, stunning in its intensity, made her chest tighten. It was as if he had gone inside, to her most inner, secret part and slowly ripped it out to examine. He had *no idea*. And he mustn't. With superhuman effort she drummed up the brittle shell of her composure, and said, 'Why not? I may as well get as much out of it as I can.'

When she saw his look of supreme...righteousness, her anger rose, swift and potent. She leant forward again.

'Tell me, did you walk into that agency and deduct a few noughts from my pay cheque once you saw how easy it would be?' She shook her head, unbelievably hurt and stung, but determined not to show it. 'Men like you disgust me. You don't know when to stop. When it's enough. Like when someone says no they mean no.'

He reached across the table so fast she couldn't escape, and he caught her hand in his. His grip was harsh, and Sorcha gasped as she felt her pulse jump straight to triple time.

'Just as you say about yourself, you know *nothing* about me. So don't presume anything.'

He looked genuinely angry, and Sorcha quailed under his fierce gaze.

'Where I come from it would be unthinkably brutal to force anyone to do anything against their will. This is a job, Sorcha—*that's all*. I've merely used a little leverage to get what I want. Tell me, is it really going to be so hard to pout and pose for a couple of weeks all around the world? To live in luxury and walk away with a few hundred thousand in your back pocket? To see a small agency benefit from the kind of exposure and money only you can bring them?'

She snatched her hand back, shaken to the core. His opinion of her was poisonous. It was tainted. She had to go—get away. She was feeling overwhelmed and seriously out of her depth. Couldn't think straight.

'I...I've lost my appetite.' The thought of eating now was making her feel sick. She stood up, picking up her jacket. Manners ingrained over years meant she couldn't just run out of the door, much as she wanted to. 'Please excuse me.'

And she turned and walked out, an awful urge to cry made her clench her jaw, lips tight together. She knew her reaction was vastly disproportionate to what had just happened. He was right. She knew that it *was* just a job, that in the end of course she could weather anything for a couple of weeks—especially if it meant her good friend got a cut. But *that* man—

A heavy hand fell on her shoulder just as she reached the doors. She whirled around jerkily, her reaction not from surprise but to his touch.

'Sorcha, I—'

'Look, I'll do your job.' She avoided looking him in the eye, tried to make her voice light to distract him from the fact that she was a quivering mass of confusion and hurt. And to feel so hurt when she barely even knew this man? It just didn't make sense. 'I've no choice, and of course you're right. How can

I turn down such a lucrative offer? After all, that *is* what I'm interested in isn't it?'

She couldn't help but look up then, but couldn't read the expression in his eyes. It wasn't what she'd expected. Not being able to read it made her feel even more panicky.

'Sorcha, look, I think we've got off to a bad—'

'Oh, don't say it—please. How could we ever have got off to a *good* start? You're the man who judged me on the basis of little more than hearsay and a grainy photograph eight years ago, who still assumes I'm walking around with track marks hidden on my body. I suppose you wouldn't believe me if I told you I've never touched a drug in my life?' She answered herself with a short harsh laugh. 'Don't bother answering. Of course not.'

She shrugged out from under his hand and moved away, closer to the door. He grabbed her wrist and, loath as she was to leave it there, because that same burning sensation was making her tingle all over, she didn't want him to see how his touch affected her. He was only trying to smooth over turbulent waters. He was a manipulator. There to make sure she toed the line, did as she was told.

She looked at him unflinchingly and her eyes were huge. The glasses were giving her a potent air of subdued sexiness that she was oblivious to. 'Just tell me where and when.'

He didn't speak for a long moment. She fought to appear cool, in control. The past was something that represented her own private hell. She knew there were parts of it, parts of *her*, that she hadn't looked at for a long time, had hoped she'd dealt with. Single-handed, this man was raking up a veritable field of emotional land mines.

'You have a week off. You'll be picked up from your apartment here in Dublin in a week's time—ten a.m. I'll send you over the schedule for the shoot.'

She nodded jerkily, finally retrieved her hand, and backed away through the door. For some bizarre reason she couldn't break her gaze from his until the last moment. Then thankfully the door opened behind her, and she slipped through and was gone.

CHAPTER FIVE

ROMAIN watched her go through the swinging doors, catching fleeting glimpses as they swung back and forth. A whole host of conflicting emotions and desires were battling under the surface of his cool grey gaze. He was watching her walk away *for the second time*.

He vowed at that moment that he would never watch her walk away again. An image crashed into his head of her lying underneath him, her sable hair spread out on a pillow, cheeks pink with arousal and passion. She was looking up, her blue eyes darkened, slumberous, and she was slowly bringing his head back down to hers, where their mouths… His whole body seemed to be igniting from the inside even as he tried to quash the picture. But its eroticism lingered. He wanted her badly. Past or no past; job or no job.

He shrugged mentally. So what if she was the first woman he'd take to bed who didn't like him, or profess to love him? For him that was the kiss of death to any relationship. He was a man who didn't deal in emotions like *like* or *love*. Their mutual antipathy could be transformed into passion. Of that he was sure. It would add an edge that was sorely lacking in his life.

He felt ruthless, almost cruel for making her do this. Then wondered broodingly if it was all an act. That effortless display of vulnerability. The hurt in her eyes when he had speculated on her motives for being involved with the outreach centre. The confusion that had assailed him when she had laughed off the suggestion that he could possibly believe she'd never been involved with drugs.

How could he be feeling in the wrong when he was offering her the kind of contract that any other model would sell their right kidney for? And why wasn't she grateful?

With an abrupt harsh movement he walked back to the table, oblivious to the covetous glances of women as he passed by. Making his apologies to the *maître d'*, he followed the path that Sorcha had just taken and, despite his reasoning to himself, as he took the lift back up to his suite he felt curiously empty. For the first time ever—despite the huge workload ahead of him, and the fact he'd be crossing the world twice in the next few days—the week seemed to stretch ahead into infinity.

The helicopter was coming in low, closer and closer to the lush green land underneath. A mark for landing materialised as if from nowhere, and to Sorcha she'd never seen anything so welcome in her life. The last forty-five minutes had been pure torture. However terrifying she found taking off in a normal-sized plane, her fear had been magnified by one hundred in this tiny machine for the duration of the journey. Her only companion, the chatty make-up artist Lucy, had happily not been able to even try and make conversation. The noise was too loud.

At last they landed. Sorcha's breathing finally returned to normal—only to shoot off the Richter scale again when she looked out of the window and saw a gleaming four-wheel drive with a tall, familiarly dark figure leaning nonchalantly against the bonnet in the near distance, arms crossed over a formidable chest. She gulped. *This was it.* No going back. Long days stretched ahead in which she was going to have to see him every day, every night and hour in between. Even though she hadn't done a location job as long as this before, she'd been away on enough shoots to know what a hothouse atmosphere it was.

As she emerged, feeling decidedly shaky—and not just from the helicopter ride—she slipped on her sunglasses. Early spring on Inis Mór, the biggest of the Aran Islands just off the west coast of Ireland, was brisk and breezy, and rare brilliant sunshine glanced off every surface. The tall figure pushed himself away from the Jeep and strolled towards her. He was even more gorgeous than she remembered, and she stumbled slightly on the bottom step. Thankfully, glasses shielded his eyes too. He was wearing jeans and a casual jumper, making him disturbingly casual, altogether more…*earthy*, *male*.

He held out his hand for her bag. 'Welcome.'

Sorcha held onto it like a lifeline and found that she couldn't utter a word. It was simply too much to be facing him again, and the hurt from their last meeting was still fresh.

His brow quirked over his glasses at the way she held onto the bag. He gestured with a hand. 'It's a beautiful location, no?'

Sorcha knew exactly how lovely it was. Not too far away, at the end of the field, a steep cliff dropped to the Atlantic Ocean, where grey-green swells with white tops battered the cliffs. Thankfully she hadn't noticed how close they'd been to the edge of the cliff, or that would have made the landing even worse. Then she saw his attention divert.

'Ah, you must be Lucy. Welcome. The crew minibus is here to take you to your lodgings. You're the last ones to arrive.'

Sorcha watched him greet Lucy, and saw the inevitable reaction as the younger girl took him in. Unbelievable. As he walked Lucy over to a minibus that Sorcha hadn't even noticed, she followed, assuming that it was for her too.

Just as she was about to get in the passenger seat, she heard a curt, 'No, Sorcha. You're coming with me.'

She turned and found he was very close behind her. She couldn't step back.

'But if I'm staying with the crew then I might as well go with Lucy.'

He shook his head. 'You're not staying with the crew. You're staying with me.'

Panic flared in her belly. 'But—'

His mouth tightened. 'And the cameramen.'

'Oh.'

She looked back for a second and saw Lucy looking from one to the other with a speculative gleam. Knowing the insidious spread of gossip on any shoot, Sorcha didn't want to be giving any fodder within minutes of landing on the island.

She slammed the door shut again behind her and smiled brightly. 'Of course—I should have guessed.' She looked back to Lucy. 'See you in the morning, no doubt…'

'You'll see each other later. We're having a dinner so that everyone can meet and get to know one another.'

And with that he bade goodbye to Lucy, took Sorcha's bag out of her white-knuckle grasp and was soon striding back to his Jeep.

She trotted after him, stupidly incensed that he could walk faster than her, and felt indignation rise at his high-handed manner. When she caught up with him he'd already stowed her bag and was holding open the passenger door. She also hated the fact that she was slightly breathless.

'I would normally stay with the crew. They're going to think it's odd if I'm with you and the photographers.'

'Worried about gossip, Sorcha?'

His disbelieving tone mocked her. After a week of telling herself that she wouldn't let him get to her, already she was failing abysmally. 'Yes, actually. Having me stay with you will be an excuse for them to think—'

'I intend to have my wicked way with you?' That supercilious brow arched again.

Sorcha's stomach clenched down low, and she reacted defensively—as if he had seen her inner turmoil, her helpless attraction. 'Of course not.' She forced herself to stop. He couldn't read her mind. 'That is…I mean, yes—they may think that.' She gave a short, unamused laugh. 'Oh, don't worry—*I* know you'd never taint yourself, touching someone like me. I've no doubt it would turn your moral stomach.'

She could feel her breasts rise up and down with her agitated breath, and hated the fact that she couldn't remain cool and unflappable in the face of his censure, as she had planned. And why wasn't he saying something? He was standing very still, and suddenly Sorcha realised that he was much closer. As if he'd moved without her realising it. Her breath hitched, and stopped altogether when a lean brown hand reached out to cup her jaw.

She felt all at once dizzy, bemused, confused, and a torrent of heat was racing upwards from her belly.

His voice was husky, had a quality that caught her on the raw. 'Actually, you're quite wrong.'

Her mouth opened. She frowned slightly. She couldn't see his eyes. And then he was gone—had stepped back and away as if the last few seconds hadn't even happened. Sorcha had to grab the door for support. She felt adrift. What had he just said? That he *would* want to touch her? Or that he knew the others would think that he wanted to have his wicked way with her? She couldn't think straight.

She heard a door slam, and a cool voice came from the interior of the Jeep. 'Well? Are you going to stand there admiring the view all day?'

Romain strode away from the door he'd just shut, behind which lay the living, breathing embodiment of his sleepless nights for the past week. Sorcha Murphy.

He had to clench his hands into fists. Seeing her emerge from the tiny helicopter less than half an hour before, he'd felt the upsurge of a desire so hot, so immediate, that he had reeled with the force of it. Her obvious reluctance to share his lodgings, albeit with others, had rankled in a way that he really didn't care for. And when he'd cupped her jaw with his hand... She had no idea how close he'd come to hauling her to him and ravaging that soft mouth. Crushing her to him.

He didn't act on basic instincts like that. In fact, although he'd desired plenty of women, not one of them had come close to igniting such forcible desire. He'd had no intention of making his needs so obvious to her, and yet he had. He hadn't ever lost control like that.

A dark, wispy memory struggled up through the

threads of his consciousness. At least not since…*then*. And that was so long ago. Would he never be free of that? And *why* was he allowing Sorcha Murphy to even evoke that memory?

Sorcha threw off the knitted shawl she'd been wearing, feeling hot and bothered, and paced the beautifully furnished bedroom with pent-up energy. She'd barely noticed the understated luxury of the old converted farmhouse. The amazing view of green fields and the huge expanse of ocean in the distance went over her head. Even the way the wild garden tapered down to a beach at the back of the house.

She'd hardly exchanged two words with Romain in the Jeep. The tension had been heavy and pulsating between them. She was still going over his words obsessively, and yet nothing in his behaviour since he'd cupped her jaw had led her to think for a second that he *did* desire her. It was as if a switch had been flicked. Once he'd shown her to her bedroom he'd curtly informed her to come back downstairs in an hour, so she could meet the others. They were to give her a briefing on the schedule for the shoot, go through the storyboards.

She sank back onto the bed. Her heart was racing. Two weeks—two weeks of suffering under his condemning looks. Could she do it?

Lisa's face flashed into her head. And also the outreach centre. In the last week, working intensively with the board at the centre, she'd realised that the money she'd earn from this job could go straight into that and would more than cover the first few months' overheads. It would mean that the centre would have absolutely every possible chance to succeed and flourish...especially as she'd been planning on her involvement being *pro bono*.

She had no choice. She was here now. For better or worse. And she would just have to keep in mind all the people who would benefit from this when things got rough.

'It's a love story...the images will run together almost like a short film.'

Sorcha choked slightly, her attention suddenly and spectacularly brought back into the huge dining room where she sat with Simon, the film cameraman, Dominic, the photographer, and Romain, who sat across the table, his huge taut body lounging against a high-backed antique chair.

The moment she'd walked into the room some minutes before, all her recent rationalising had fled out of the window. Her entire focus had been taken by him—again. She'd noticed in a flash that he'd just had a shower. The clean crisp scent had hit her so strongly that she'd imagined everyone must be able to smell it. His hair was still damp, furrowed from where he'd obviously run fingers through it. And yet when she'd looked at him he'd been practically glacial, those grey eyes as cold as the nearby ocean.

She caught herself and modulated her tone. 'I'm sorry, Simon, can you say that again?'

The cameraman was a nice guy. From London. Good looking, a little cocky, dressed in a very trendily casual way. But he didn't come close to the class that Romain exuded so effortlessly. And she hated that she'd noticed that.

'As Simon said, the stills will run as one campaign and the film will be shown in a series of thirty-second commercials, the sequence building up the story.'

Reluctantly she looked to Romain, who had spoken. So far the photographer hadn't said anything. But Sorcha knew him well from years ago. He'd been on the periphery of the group she'd hung out with for that brief, yet catastrophic time, and although he hadn't been directly involved she hadn't mistaken the knowing, mocking glance in his eyes. She knew his type, and usually steered well clear. It seemed, however, as if she wouldn't be able to get too far away this time.

She sighed. The weeks ahead were becoming more challenging than she could ever have imagined.

She deliberately focused her attention on Simon, the least threatening of the men in the room at that moment. 'I'm sorry, would you mind explaining a little more?'

He smiled with an infectious grin, which she welcomed as an antidote to the tension she felt. She struggled to concentrate.

'We follow you as you're led on a romantic trail,

of sorts, around the world. It'll be a sumptuous, truly global love story. In each place the relationship goes to another level. We see you meet, fall in love, even get married, and it's all going to be shot with a very moody, dreamlike feel. The last shot will show you and your lover with a family.'

Sorcha's head spun. She couldn't look at Romain. For some reason she felt ridiculously exposed— almost as though someone had gone into her deepest fantasies and converted them into a script. And since when had she ever seen herself with a happy family? After the devastation of lies and truths that had followed her father's death, she'd had a cynical and somewhat jaded view of so-called happy families, distrusting anyone who professed to be part of one. As she and her brother could attest, their realities had been anything but happy.

After a few more minutes going over what they hoped to achieve at this location, Sorcha got up to leave, relieved when it didn't look as though Romain was going to follow her. He did, however, remind her that dinner would be held in that dining room for all the crew at eight sharp that evening.

She was breathing a sigh of relief when she reached the door, but it didn't last long when she realised that Dominic was right behind her. He came too close, crowding her as she went through the door, and she automatically stepped away. Everything about him was making some part of her crawl. He wasn't a bad-looking man—in fact she knew that many would find

·his boyish looks a turn-on—but he left Sorcha feeling cold. He didn't take her hint, and fell into step beside her. She cursed herself for heading outside and not upstairs, to the sanctuary of her room.

'Nice to see you again, Sorch…it's been years, hasn't it? Although I'm sure you remember the good old days… Pity you couldn't handle the pace…'

She deliberately kept her voice light, giving him the briefest of glances. 'Yes, it has been years, Dominic… It's nice to see you too. I'm going to go for a walk, so if you don't mind…'

As she went to walk away, towards the front door, she felt her arm being taken in a none too gentle grip. She whirled around in shock. 'What do you—?'

Dominic was smiling, but it wasn't friendly. 'I *do* remember the good old days. I remember Christian…don't you? I saw him recently. When I told him we were working together he told me all about you.' He looked her up and down. 'I'm looking forward to getting to know you better—and if you're looking for anything…*anything* at all…you know where to find me.'

Sorcha felt disgust and fear fill her belly. She knew exactly what he was talking about. Drugs. She refused to let him bring her back down the path of her dark memories. She pulled her arm free with effort.

'I'd prefer it if you called me Sorcha. And I won't be looking for anything at all. I'm here to work. Now, please—'

At that moment she caught a flash of movement

in the hall behind Dominic, and saw Romain coming out of the room. She saw him take in the way she was standing so close to Dominic, and imagined that it must look intimate. Without knowing where the desire was coming from she suddenly wanted to make it very clear that it wasn't. But what could she say or do?

That familiar glower was on his face, and he called curtly for Dominic to come back into the room. Sorcha took advantage and fled out into the sunshine, away from the dark heat of censure in his eyes.

That evening Sorcha looked at the clothes she'd laid out on the bed. Even though tonight wasn't a formal occasion, she itched to put on something that would assert cool professionalism. Romain scrambled her brain, her senses, and she needed all the armour she could muster. She'd been lacking in control ever since she'd come face to face with him in New York, and it had to stop or she'd never get through the job.

She reached for jeans and flat ballet pumps, and a soft cashmere wraparound cardigan. It didn't need anything underneath, but the sensual feel of the fabric—*why did it suddenly have to feel sensual?*—made her team it with a plain white vest top. The deep sapphire colour of the cardigan made her eyes a dark smoky blue. Pulling her hair back and up, she clipped it haphazardly. Stuck on her glasses. She looked at her image, somewhere between a sixteen-year-old cheerleader and a student.

Sticking her tongue out at herself, she ignored the two spots of bright colour on her cheeks and left the room, only to walk smack-bang into a hard, unyielding chest.

CHAPTER SIX

THE wind was driven out of her more as a result of her reaction to coming into contact with his hard chest than because of the impact. Sorcha looked up with dazed eyes. Big hands encircled her upper arms and she could feel his body heat enveloping her. They were so close that all she'd have to do was stretch up slightly and her mouth would be close enough to—

With an almost violent movement she pulled free and jerked away, rubbing her arms. She glowered at Romain, who stuck his hands in the pockets of his dark trousers and leant against the doorjamb. A dark shirt made him look dangerous, foreign, in the gloom of the corridor. The grey of his eyes stood out.

Nervously she touched a hand to her glasses. 'Do you always lurk outside people's doors? Or were you just afraid I was turning my room into a den of iniquity?'

A smile quirked his mouth up at one side, making him look even more rakishly handsome. She wasn't ready to face him—had been counting on the space, however brief, between her room and the dining room to gather herself.

'I was merely coming to escort you downstairs. Everyone is here.'

'I'm quite capable of walking myself down some stairs.'

He fell into step beside her. She wanted to turn away from his presence but the corridor was old and tiny.

'Prickly, aren't you? I hope this means you're a morning person.'

She scowled at him briefly and preceded him down the stairs.

Romain followed with a thoughtful look on his face. His jaw tightened as his eyes were drawn to the sway of her bottom in the tight, faded jeans. The force of her cannoning into him had shocked him too. Or rather, the feel of her soft breasts crushed against his chest had shocked him—with how badly he'd wanted to walk her back into the room and shut the door behind them.

In the large drawing room everyone was gathered, drinking aperitifs. Local girls in black trousers and white shirts walked through with canapés. Sorcha was relieved to see some familiar faces—and one in particular.

'Sorcha, you gorgeous girl, come here!'

She was grabbed around the waist and lifted high by a tall, handsome man—the hairstylist. When he finally put her down she was laughing and red-faced. 'Val! You nearly stopped the blood supply to my middle region.'

'How is the smartest model in the world?' He pretended to think for a second. 'Now, was it a first, or a second? I can't remember…'

Sorcha punched him playfully. 'It was Summa Cum Laude to be precise, but really it's not that amazing, lots of people got the same mark.'

He looked mock-shocked. 'Maybe so, but you came in the top five of your class, girlfriend. If that isn't—'

'What's this?'

Sorcha's back straightened. For a brief moment she'd forgotten Romain was right behind her. How much had he heard?

Before she could stop him, Val was fluttering his lashes in his campest mode and chattering with scant regard for discretion. 'Our girl here has just graduated with flying colours from—'

'Val, you never showed me your wedding ring.'

Acting on a panicked impulse, desperately counting on Val's extreme yet lovable self-absorption, Sorcha breathed a sigh of relief when he promptly forgot about relaying her news and proceeded to show off the heavy platinum band, regaling them with stories about his recent marriage in London to his boyfriend. This was all punctuated with hot, heavy looks at Romain, who Sorcha could see was completely unfazed. She'd seen other men driven almost to violence by Val's unwanted flirtatious attentions, but Romain was so sure of himself that he was totally at ease, bantering back and forth. It made a funny feeling lodge in her chest.

Val got distracted by someone and walked away just as a bell sounded for dinner. Sorcha already felt wrung out. She made to move, but was blocked by Romain's tall body.

'What did you stop Val telling me?'

She should have known he wouldn't let it go—and she *had* diverted Val with all the subtlety of a brick. Hemmed in between a chair and Romain, she could see everyone filing out to the dining room across the hall and looked after them wistfully.

'Nothing.' She sounded evasive.

'What was he talking about, and why did you distract him from telling me?'

Why was she feeling so self-protective? It wouldn't mean anything if she told him…if anything it might make him respect her more. She opened her mouth. Nothing came out. She didn't want to tell him because she didn't want him to know anything about her. And if he knew this…well, it might make him curious about other things. She needed to keep him at a distance. And then she remembered his scathing response to her involvement with the outreach centre.

She looked up and held her gaze to his, even though it wasn't easy. That intense grey seemed to enmesh her every sense. The room was silent. Everyone was gone, and again it was just the two of them. She willed ice into her eyes and into her veins, which seemed to be far too heated of late.

'He was talking about something that would be of no interest to you. It was personal and private, and he'd forgotten that I'd asked him not to mention it to anyone, that's all. Anyway, how could you possibly be interested in anything about me?'

'Oh, but I am, Sorcha—*very* interested. You're mine for the next two weeks. And you're an expensive commodity.'

Her eyes blazed with sudden fury, and she hated the frisson that had skittered down her spine at the way he'd said '*very* interested'.

'That does not give you the right to pry. I told you before—stay out of my private life.'

His face came close to hers. 'The hell I will—especially if you're thinking of getting cosy with Dominic…'

She reared back. 'What?'

'I saw you two earlier.'

'You saw nothing.'

'I saw—'

'Come on, you two. We're all waiting to eat!'

Sorcha jerked her head round to see Val at the door, with a curious look on his face.

Romain was smooth, as if he got caught in heated dialogue every day. He gestured for Sorcha to precede him from the room, and her legs felt shaky as she did so. She avoided Val's eye, knowing full well that there'd be a very questioning look on his face. He knew her well enough to know that she didn't get into heated debates with gorgeous men.

Dinner provided a brief respite. Sorcha found herself seated next to Lucy, who was as chatty as ever, and Simon. He was busy explaining the logistics of how they would be shooting. She couldn't, however, be unaware of the man on the opposite side of the huge table. Every now and then she'd feel a prickling sensation on her neck and look up, only to find that Romain would be deep in conversation with the stylist, Claire, who had grabbed a seat beside him with more haste than grace.

She couldn't mistake the proprietorial manner in which the older woman, who was very attractive with her short blonde bob, was monopolising Romain's attention, and Sorcha sent up silent thanks. But then a little dart of something made her acutely aware of the exact moment when Claire laid her hand on Romain's arm and Sorcha had the bizarrest impulse to go and knock it off, feeling suddenly incensed, as if his arm was *her* personal property. She closed her eyes weakly.

'Are you all right, Sorcha?'

Her eyes snapped open. Simon was looking at her with concern. She smiled quickly. 'Fine. Absolutely fine.' She mustered up a fake yawn. 'Just a bit tired. It's been a long day.'

'Yes. And it'll be even longer tomorrow. They want to try and get a lot done in one day.'

Back in the drawing room for after-dinner drinks a short time later, Sorcha circulated and got to know the group of about eight people. She knew that by the end of the shoot they'd all know each other much more intimately, having been thrust together for hours on end every day.

They seemed on the whole like a nice bunch, and she found to her surprise that she was looking forward to the shoot. The only person she'd avoided, apart from Romain, from whom she'd carefully made sure she was always on the opposite side of the room, had been Dominic. Contrary to what Romain might believe, Dominic had obviously set Lucy the young make-up artist in his sights, and the two had slipped away somewhere. Sorcha was quite happy, wanting to have as little to do with him as possible.

Later that night she lay in the dark, staring up at the ceiling. She'd made her excuses early and had crept away to bed.

This is a job like any other. Be cool, be calm, be professional and everything will be OK.

She kept telling herself that. She could handle anything. Anyone. Even Romain.

But as she turned over and tried to go to sleep, the only image in her brain was the one of his face as she'd left the room earlier. It had held that same intensity when she'd walked away from him in New York. As if he could see right into her soul… And that was crazy. He was the last man in the world she wanted looking anywhere near her soul…

The next day they started early. Simon wanted to get a dawn shot of Sorcha on the beach. Dressed very impractically, in a long silk diaphanous dress, she kept a parka on until the last moment, and tried not to show how cold she was in the chilly early-morning air.

All the shot called for was for her to walk along the seashore, find a bottle in the sand and pick it up. The idea was that the bottle held a message, which she would read and which would lead her to the next place…and so on.

Standing shivering, waiting for Simon and Dominic to set up, Sorcha sent up silent thanks that at least on set Dominic seemed to be professional enough not to allude to anything, as he had the day before.

'Sorcha…'

Romain.

She'd managed to avoid looking at him, but even so she was well aware of his location at every moment, and now he was right beside her. She turned reluctantly.

'Yes?'

Romain looked down at her and his insides contracted. He didn't think he'd ever seen anyone so gorgeous, cheeks reddened by the chill wind, long hair loose and wild. Her eyes shone with a fierce, vivid blue and he almost forgot what he'd come to say. And that made him feel short-tempered. It also made him sound clipped.

'We've decided to do a part of the sequence here that we were going to do in India. It's a shot that includes Zane…your counterpart.'

Sorcha frowned. Zane was the male model/actor due to play her lover.

'But Zane doesn't start till we get to New York. He's not here.'

'I'm aware of that fact. But, as Simon pointed out, I'm similar in height and colouring, at least from behind, so I'll stand in for him.'

Alarm bells went zinging off in Sorcha's head, and she looked at him suspiciously, 'What does the shot involve?'

A dark light came into Romain's eyes, confusing Sorcha. Everything around them had faded into the background.

'You and me...' he drawled.

Sorcha fought to contain panic and snapped out, 'Yes, well, even *I* could have deduced that—'

Just then Dominic called for her to step onto her mark. She glared at Romain, who was looking far too smug at her obvious discomfiture.

Sorcha found out more at lunchtime, and she mulled it all over in her head as she took off for a brief solitary walk afterwards. It turned out that the shot Romain had told her about had to be done at sunset, and Claire the stylist had already flown back to Dublin to get the dress required, as it was meant to be part of the wedding sequence. That had made Sorcha's nerves go completely. She'd been too scared to ask what exactly was involved.

Would she have to *kiss him*?

That thought sent all sorts of shivers through her, and not all of them were of disgust...or trepidation. Was he doing this on purpose, just to mess with her?

She berated herself. Now she was just being silly.

CHAPTER SEVEN

A FEW hours later, feeling very nervous, Sorcha stood on the shoreline again, this time in a simple knee-length white broderie anglaise dress from an exclusive designer. It was meant to be a wedding dress. Her hair was up in a loose knot, and a white orchid was tucked behind her ear.

Claire the stylist was muttering as she secured the dress at the back. 'You would not believe the pressure I was under to get back here… And this dress—it's not even been on the catwalk yet. We weren't meant to be shooting it for another week. It had to come from Paris with a courier *and* a bodyguard. And now you're the one that gets to be held in Romain's arms…*honestly…*'

Held in his arms? Sorcha's insides froze. Surely she just meant with his arm around her shoulders as they looked out at the sunset?

And then he was there, striding towards her. He wore a white tuxedo shirt that was open at the neck, a bow tie dangling untied. His black trousers were rolled up to the knee, showing off strong, shapely calf muscles. She felt weak.

The sun was setting over the horizon, and the mood of the crew was getting more frantic, with Simon and Dominic shouting out orders as they worked simultaneously. Romain came and stood before her, slanting a look down her body, taking in her long, slim, very pale legs.

'Very sweet—almost virginal, in fact.'

Sorcha felt a familiar secret pain grip her. She had so much to hide from a man like this.

'Let's just get on with it, shall we?' she bit out.

And in the next instant her world was upended and she was lifted against a broad, strong and very hard chest. Immediately and instinctively her arms had to go around his neck. Wide, surprised eyes clashed with his.

'What the—?'

Romain felt the rigidity in her body. 'Hush. We're meant to be in love.'

'Don't make me sick! And if this is your idea of a joke—'

Simon came over and held a light meter close to Sorcha's face, making her shut her mouth abruptly.

'That's great, guys. Let me know if you need a break, Romain. You'll need to stand there for a while.'

Simon walked away and Sorcha smiled sweetly at Romain. 'I do hope I'm not too heavy for you?'

'Not at all,' he said lightly. 'Like the proverbial feather.'

His arms did feel secure around her—not a tremor.

And Sorcha knew well that she wasn't exactly small. She always ate well, but had been lucky enough to inherit a metabolism that burnt off calories quickly. Still, she was no lightweight. The fact that Romain seemed to be holding her so effortlessly made her feel small and feminine, *delicate* for the first time in her life.

She sighed deeply and looked out to sea. But as she sighed, her breasts moved against his chest. She stopped breathing as her nipples reacted and tightened.

His mouth came close to her ear and he whispered softly, his accent pronounced. 'It helps if you breathe...'

She turned her head, and the retort on her lips was quickly forgotten. Their heads were so close together that she could feel his breath reach out and mingle with her own. She saw the deeper flecks of grey in his eyes, the small lines that fanned out from the corners of his eyes, and that suddenly made her want to see him laugh, to see how they crinkled up.

Surrounded in a bubble of sensation, Sorcha couldn't deny it any longer—not when she was held so tight against him. This man had broken through the wall that she'd built around her sexuality. He was smashing it down with what seemed to be little more than that proverbial feather.

Her other hand was somewhere around his shoulder. It had been in the act of pushing him away. But now the feel of his warm skin underneath the shirt was acting like a magnet. Completely unaware of what was going on around them, but perhaps subconsciously knowing that it might be sanctioned, Sorcha's hand moved up of its own volition to his neck.

In a completely untutored and sensuous move that had Romain's heart-rate soaring, Sorcha allowed the back of her hand to drift up his neck, pushing aside the open collar of his shirt. And then, her eyes following the movement as though mesmerised, her hand drifted upwards until her palm rested on his lightly stubbled jaw.

Romain stared down into her face. He willed her eyes to meet his, and as if she could hear him they did. A silken cord had wrapped itself around his every sense and he felt himself tighten and harden. She had become soft and pliant in his arms, her curves moulding to his form like a jigsaw piece slotting into place.

All Sorcha could see was his mouth. Her thumb moved closer, traced the corner of his lower lip. They were so close. And then his head dipped slightly. She felt his breath feather again. Her eyelids felt heavy and started to flutter closed. Every part of her was aching to feel that mouth on hers…

'Very good! And do you know what? We don't even need to see a kiss. I think this works really well…'

Simon's voice cut through the haze of sensuality that had been clouding Sorcha's brain like an alarm going off. She actually flinched—a minor movement, but one which had Romain gripping her tight to him again. But this time she held herself stiff and would not look at him. *God.* What on earth must he think? They'd been shooting all the time and Sorcha hadn't even noticed!

Romain felt dazed…out of sync as he put Sorcha down until her feet touched the ground. Surrounded by all the crew, he couldn't do what he wanted and keep her close, take that lush mouth as he'd been so close to doing. The way she'd been looking at him just then… He felt limbless. Had he just been taken for a complete fool?

After what seemed like aeons, he put her away from him with two hands. She was very shaky.

His mouth was hard, his face taut. 'You're a good actress.'

She looked up quickly and saw the harshness there, twisting his mouth.

Acting?

Well, if that was what he thought…thank God.

She forced a smile from somewhere and left the protection of his hands. Thankfully she didn't fall at his feet, and with a briskness she certainly didn't feel she said, 'It's my job. What you hired me for.'

And on very shaky limbs she walked over to the others and the protection of the busyness of the crew as they packed up.

The next day they were due to do a couple of quick shots in the morning and then travel to New York in the afternoon. Sorcha had tossed and turned all night, unable to get the memory of being in Romain's arms out of her mind…her body. Giving up at six a.m., seeing the first light of dawn, she got out of bed. She knew what would calm her.

She put on her running clothes—a long sleeved T-shirt and jogging bottoms. Her battered sneakers. She tried to jog wherever she was, finding it to be almost like a form of meditation as well as exercise. She met no one on her way outside, and pulled back her sleep-mussed hair into a ponytail, heading for the beach. The air was crisp and fresh and blue skies promised another beautiful spring day, which in the west of Ireland was an anomaly to be savoured.

Hitting the beach, she found that it was pleasingly much bigger and longer than she'd expected, stretching away a few miles into the distance. After some warming up she set out at a steady pace. The repetition of movement, the control of her breath, all transported her away from disturbing thoughts and images.

About forty minutes later, feeling much calmer and very smug with herself, she came back closer to the house and stopped to rest at the seashore. Impulsively she took off her shoes and socks, wanting to feel the cold sting of the Atlantic on her hot feet. She contemplated going back to get her one-piece, knowing that the initial pain of the icy water would be far outweighed by the exhilarating feeling afterwards. As she stood debating whether or not to go back and get her suit, she looked out to sea and something caught her attention. Someone swimming.

Powerful arms scissoring in and out of the water, a glimpse of a strong, olive-skinned back.

Her breath hitched and stopped. It could only be one person. No one else had that physique. And she knew that it would take more than average strength first of all to brave the icy Atlantic and then to swim in it. The currents were sometimes lethal. Mesmerised by his grace and beauty, she couldn't move. And then, too late, she realised that he'd been coming closer all the time. The arms stopped and he stood waist-deep in the sea, water streaming off a perfectly muscled torso. Like some kind of god, he emerged from the waves, and the unreality of it all made Sorcha feel as if she was in some kind of dream.

It was only when he was walking out of the water, showing a broad chest that tapered into a slim waist, dark shorts which clung to powerful thigh muscles rippling under bronzed skin, that Sorcha finally seemed to come to her senses. The sleepless night had obviously taken its toll. She was standing there like some kind of drooling groupie!

With a strangled gasp, she turned and picked up her shoes and socks, about to make a hasty retreat. She hadn't counted on his speed.

'Wait.'

She stopped in her tracks. The serenity of the morning was gone. Her heart hammered anew, and it wasn't from the exercise. She turned to face him and tried to look as blank as possible. It was hard. Romain stood just feet away, hands on hips, chest rising and falling, salt water sluicing off his skin, his hair plastered to a well-shaped skull.

'Enjoying the view?'

She coloured in an instant and Romain frowned. *The outraged virgin?* Where had that come from? Just another aspect of Sorcha's chameleon-like personality. He could see the way she held herself…so stiff…but when he'd been coming out from the water, when he'd seen her first, she'd had a look of something close to exultation on her face.

'Don't be ridiculous. I was out jogging. And I was merely making sure you were OK. I didn't know who was swimming, and the currents here can be strong.'

He picked up a towel from nearby. She hadn't even noticed it. 'Would you have saved me if I'd got into trouble?'

Sorcha snorted inelegantly. 'What do you think?'

He rubbed at his hair, totally unconcerned by her comment. With his face obscured momentarily, she couldn't halt the inevitable slide of her gaze downwards again, seeing how the cold water had made his nipples hard. Her own seemed to pucker and tighten in direct response, and she hurriedly crossed her arms over the thin material of her T-shirt.

'It *was* amazing.' He jerked his head back towards the pounding waves.

Sorcha was distracted for a second, that sexy accent making her breath hitch again. And she did envy him the experience, knowing well how he must be feeling right now—the rush of endorphins, the tingling sensations as life came back into a body that would be near frozen.

'I know.' She sounded wistful. 'It's been a while since I swam in the sea here, but I remember.'

'Nothing stopping you now. You could go in in your underwear. I can keep an eye.'

The lightness in his voice didn't fool her for a second. And if he thought she was going to strip off in front of him...

She shook her head and watched with widening eyes as he proceeded to hitch the towel around his waist and strip off his shorts underneath. At the last second she whirled away from him.

'Do you mind?'

Romain studied her taut back. Just who *was* Sorcha Murphy?

'I'm decent again.'

Sorcha turned around reluctantly, relieved to see him buttoning up his jeans—although that led her eyes to his hands, and the line of dark hair that snaked up to his chest. A worn sweatshirt abruptly concealed him from view and she felt saggy with relief.

He strolled towards her nonchalantly. 'So, why don't you?'

She frowned, her head feeling muggy, unconsciously backing away 'What?'

'Go for a swim.'

She shook her head again. 'No.' And she struck off up the beach.

He kept pace with her all too easily.

She looked at him sideways, it seemed silly not to admit the truth. 'But you're right...I did think of it. I was going to go back inside and get my swimsuit.'

'Coward,' he called softly.

She avoided his eye, afraid of what she'd see, and looked at her watch. They were at the back of the house, a huge hedge obscuring them from view. 'As I have to be in make-up in less than half an hour, I'm sure you don't want to be encouraging me to be late?'

He spread an arm wide for her to precede him up the path and dipped his head. 'Of course you're right.'

She went to squeeze past him. The narrow gate was too small for two people, and he wasn't budging an inch. Sorcha gritted her teeth, not even breathing, but even so she could feel his chest. She imagined it would still be cold from the sea...and were his nipples still hard?

She felt like screaming inwardly. Until she'd met him in New York, thoughts like this had never entered her head. She didn't know if he was doing it deliberately, just to unsettle her, or because he—

Two arms came round her at that moment, and her heart skidded to a halt.

The feel of her lithe, athletic, yet lush body was too much for him. He was only human, and he couldn't wait any more. Not after the extreme erotic torture of holding her in his arms yesterday and his sleepless night last night.

She looked up, panic-stricken. 'What do you think you're—'

'Something I've wanted to do ever since I saw you across that room in New York, and more especially since yesterday... What we would have done if we hadn't been interrupted.'

His powerful arms held her captive. She couldn't move, and to do so would be to invite a friction between their bodies the thought of which made scorched colour enter Sorcha's already pink cheeks. His words and her own body's reaction scared the life out of her, but something joyous moved through her too, and that scared her even more witless.

She had to do something!

His head dipped, and she tried in vain to push with her hands.

'Aren't you afraid you might catch some immoral disease?'

His mouth hovered just inches away... Sorcha knew she should turn her head away—so why didn't she? Her eyes, big as saucers, gazed up into his.

Romain felt his whole body tighten, felt fire blazing a trail along every vein and artery, pumping blood to areas that were becoming painfully engorged. He couldn't even take in her words, or answer with any coherence.

Before Sorcha could move or stop him his head had dipped. The morning disappeared. Mad insanity arrived. Insanity that tasted delicious...like nothing she'd ever dreamt of before. This was a kiss unlike any other she'd experienced. The first press of his lips to hers was benedictory, almost reverent, and then he drew back. She opened her eyes. When had she closed them? And how had her hands crept up to his neck? The stark reality of what she was doing washed through her and she struggled again, but Romain was ruthless. He pushed her back against the gate, trapped her completely with his hard body.

'No, you don't… You want this just as much as me…'

'No!' she panted,. 'I don—'

And this time there was no gentle. He was hard, intrusive, ruthless, and determined to break through her every defence. His tongue forced her mouth open, made a bold foray into her mouth, and though she first had an instinct to bite…it turned quickly into a desire to explore, touch and taste. He tasted of salt water. His hand was on the back of her head, angling her better for his satisfaction. She gave a deep mewl in her throat and her treacherous hands climbed again, finding the way the skin grew silky around the back of his neck, where his wet hair made her think of him emerging from the sea just moments ago. That had a tight spiral of need starting in her belly and rising upwards, consuming every part of her on the way.

Her breasts felt sore, aching heavily against the thin material of her T-shirt and bra. She pressed herself closer, lost in a maelstrom of passion so dizzyingly new and overwhelming that she couldn't even question it. Romain's other hand smoothed down her back, all the way to her bottom, where he cupped one cheek, pressing her even closer, and all the time their mouths clung, tongues duelling in a frantic building heat that threatened to combust around them.

It was a dog barking that finally cut through the insanity that had taken them over. Romain noticed before she did, and pulled back with extreme reluctance. His eyes darted to a dune nearby, and he contemplated taking her right now, right there…the aching in his loins crying out for immediate release. But a dog would have an owner, and now was not the time or place. Something triumphant moved through him when he looked down into slightly glazed blue eyes. He'd been right. But when he'd sensed passion under that pale skin he hadn't dreamt how incendiary it was. He smiled.

Sorcha finally reacted to his smile. It was smug…and something else. It made her heart turn over and at the same time her blood run cold. This time she pushed and he let her go. She fought to control her breathing, her hammering heart, and looked at him, trying not to let the confusion she felt show on her face.

'I don't know what you thought that was, but it won't be happening again.'

She turned to walk away and he caught her back, catching her off guard. She fell against his body, and desire coiled tight in her abdomen again.

'Yes, it will. And next time we won't be interrupted.'

It was only then that Sorcha even noticed movement on the beach and saw someone walking their dog. Mortification twisted her insides. She glared back up at Romain.

'You might think that every model in the world wants you to bed them, but believe me, *I* don't. I haven't changed my opinion of you, and you're the last man on this earth that I'd want to sleep with.'

Before he could come back with some silky-smooth retort, with flaming cheeks she pulled free and ran back into the house.

CHAPTER EIGHT

LATER that day, as Sorcha boarded the privately chartered jet, it felt as if aeons had passed. Those moments on the beach, that kiss, had an intimate residue that made Sorcha feel skittish. And, to her utter dismay, she saw that the only free seat was beside Romain.

She hovered reluctantly for a second by the empty seat. Romain glanced up eventually from some papers in his lap. He looked more like the successful businessman now, in a dark suit, light shirt and tie, undone slightly, with a top button open. A glimpse of the strong column of brown throat was tantalising.

'It seems as though this is the only free seat.'

He smiled wolfishly. 'Please, be my guest. It'll be fun to watch you try to squirm away from me for five hours.'

Sorcha sat down gingerly, very careful about where she put her arms. Then she sat back and closed her eyes.

Before long, though, the familiar terror began making its all too predictable insidious climb inside her chest as the engine's throttle roared. At this moment even Romain beside her couldn't distract her from it. She heard him rattle papers. The engines started up in earnest, the plane lurched forward, and she felt the colour drain from her face. Her hands, despite her efforts not to give anything away were clenched tightly in her lap. She longed to be able to wrap them around the seat—that always made her feel stupidly protected—but she didn't want to draw attention to herself.

As the plane gathered speed down the runway, her heart beat faster and faster.

'What's wrong? Scared of flying?'

The voice came from right beside her ear, and Sorcha jumped, eyes opening wide as she looked to Romain. She couldn't even speak, and just nodded silently. When he saw the truly blatant fear in the blue depths, any teasing fled Romain's mind. He acted purely on instinct and took one of Sorcha's hands in his. It was clenched tight and he had to prise the bloodless fingers apart. Finally he was able to thread his fingers with hers and grip her tight. He saw her other hand go in a white-knuckle grip to the armrest.

Sorcha couldn't believe it. The mind-numbing fear, the awful acrid taste of it, wasn't hitting her as hard as it normally did. The plane left the ground, that awful moment came…and it was still awful, but for the first time ever bearable. It was only then, as the fear began its slow decline, that Sorcha felt the long warm fingers entwined with hers and heat unfurled in her belly. She looked down and could see white and brown fingers in a tangle. A hot, tight feeling made her abdomen clench, and the kiss invaded her consciousness with full lurid recall.

Looking up to Romain with horror, she saw him wincing. Abruptly she loosened her grip, but he didn't loosen his. His face cleared, though, and he smiled.

'Remind me never to arm-wrestle you. I don't think I'd win.'

Sorcha snatched her hand back. She felt acutely vulnerable. She couldn't believe she'd been so weakly transparent.

He settled back comfortably, turning his big body towards her. Sorcha looked resolutely at the back of the seat in front of her.

'So is it just the take-off, or the whole thing?'

She sighed deeply. 'Just the take off.' She looked at him warily. 'And being in tiny helicopters.' She gave a delicate shudder. 'That trip to Inis Mor…'

'I thought you looked unnaturally pale when you got off. Why didn't you say anything?'

She shrugged, casting him a quick glance. 'What's the point? It's just a silly fear. No need to cause a fuss.'

He felt anger lick through him, but not directed at her. 'So you'd prefer to put yourself through moments of terror like that just to keep people happy?'

'Well, how else would I have got over there—or anywhere, these days?'

He just looked at her broodingly. 'Where did it come from?'

Her head had that fuzzy feeling again. Why couldn't she look this man in the eye for longer than two seconds without her head going to mush? He was going to suspect she was certifiably stupid.

'What?'

'Your fear of flying...taking off...do you know where it comes from?'

Sorcha nodded slowly. Weighed up what it would mean to tell him. He saw the hesitation, and she saw how his jaw tightened.

'I forgot about the embargo on your private life.'

Despite her best instincts, at that moment she perversely wanted to put her hand on his arm. She clenched her hand into a fist again. 'No,' she said tightly, and then, with a small smile that made her feel as if she'd been invaded by a rogue body snatcher, she said, 'It's fine.'

She looked away for a second, and then back, struck by how, even though they were in the plane surrounded by the crew, it felt as though it was just them, in some kind of bubble.

'I was three years old, and we were taking a trip back to Spain to visit my mother's family—'

He looked at her incredulously. 'You're Spanish?'

She hesitated for a split second... *Hadn't she been for most of her life?* 'Half-Spanish... My mother is. My father is—*was* Irish...'

'He's dead?'

She nodded, and felt herself go cold inside, she knew she was lying about being half-Spanish, but that was a part of her that was certainly out of bounds for discussion and none of his business. That bit of information lay far too close to the truth of everything else.

'He died just before I turned seventeen.'

'I'm sorry.'

Romain saw how she'd changed in an instant from being lukewarm to icy cool. He wouldn't have believed it if he hadn't seen it with his own eyes.

'It was a long time ago.'

'My father died when I was twelve…a heart attack.'

She looked at him, that guarded expression faltering slightly. She remembered what Maud had told her about his mother. 'Mine too…a heart attack, I mean. I'm sorry.'

A moment passed between them, and neither noticed for a second when the air stewardess asked if they wanted anything. Then Sorcha looked up and a guilty flush stained her cheeks. What was she thinking? Getting lost in his eyes, telling him about her father? She saw the way the stewardess practically ate him alive with just a look and welcomed the cold dose of reality.

When they'd ordered water, she could feel him settle back in.

Please, no more conversation…

'So…your fear of flying…'

Sorcha's tone was brisk and almost bored. She didn't see the way Romain's eyes narrowed on her speculatively.

'Like I said, we were on holiday, going to Spain. It's really not that exciting—'

'Indulge me.'

Sorcha gulped, looked at him quickly, and then away again. 'The plane had just taken off, and at the last second something failed and it crashed back down. I didn't have my belt on.' She grimaced. 'I'd managed to unlock it somehow, and when the plane fell back down like a stone I fell and got thrown around a bit…' She shrugged. 'That's it. I told you it was nothing to get worked up about. It's silly to still let it affect me.'

He looked at her for a long, intense moment and couldn't stop the feeling that he was somehow letting her get to him—get under his skin in a way that went beyond physical attraction. He drew back. The shutters came down, his face expressionless.

'If you don't mind, I have an important meeting when we land in New York and I need to concentrate on some paperwork.'

And he promptly shut Sorcha out as effectively as she had shut him out from the start. It threw her. She made the motions of getting a book out of her bag, put on her glasses to read…but the page and the print blurred in front of her eyes. She couldn't relax next to Romain, and her mind was feverishly trying to decipher what had made him clam up like that.

She was intrigued. Suddenly *he* had more facets to him than a mere autocratic and judgmental luxury goods magnate. She recalled how professional he'd been on the set the day before. He'd run it smoothly, fairly…especially when Dominic had threatened to throw a little tantrum when something hadn't gone his way. Sorcha wasn't used to a steadying force on a set. She found more often than not that *she* acted as the peacemaker, the mediator between various hysterical egos.

She sneaked another look, but Romain was a million miles away, immersed in facts and figures, shirtsleeves rolled up, his profile harshly beautiful. And extremely remote. In that moment she had trouble believing that he had ever kissed her with such passion only that morning.

Some time later Sorcha felt a bump and her head jerked up. She'd been asleep on something very soft…it felt like a cushion…only it was no cushion. It was an arm and a very broad chest. She jerked upright completely. Slumberous hooded grey eyes looked back at her, completely unconcerned. Sorcha took it all in in a flash—along with the fact that they were about to land. She must have heard the wheels being lowered.

The seat divide was up, and Romain had leant back into his own reclined seat, pulling her with him onto his chest. The sudden memory of how he'd felt underneath her cheek made a flush spread through her body.

'I…' She couldn't speak.

Romain watched her flounder. She looked sleepy and tousled and flushed and so…gorgeous that he had to shift minutely in his seat. He'd suffered the ignominy of his body reacting against the will he'd tried to impose on it for the past three hours or so, and right now he felt he needed to take a very long, very cold shower. When Sorcha's head had kept drooping in jerks as she'd slept, he'd put down his papers, unbuckled their belts and pulled her into him. Again, he'd been surprised at how her soft curves had seemed to melt into his body, as if made for him. Her evocative scent had drifted up from silky black hair.

Their seats were towards the front, and somewhat screened from the rest of the cabin. And it was that fact now that seemed to be uppermost on Sorcha's mind as her hair swung around her shoulders in an arc and she cast a nervous look backwards.

'No one saw,' he offered helpfully, feeling absurdly annoyed.

She sat back and folded her arms. 'I didn't mean to fall asleep. I must've been more tired than I realised.'

She could see him shrug out of the corner of her eye as he flipped his seat upright, 'The pleasure was all mine.'

She burned. Her insides were on fire. She couldn't even escape and go to the toilet as they were about to land. Buckling her belt again, she busied herself putting her book away—but not before it had fallen out of her hands and into Romain's lap. He picked it up before she had a chance to snatch it back.

'*Man and His Symbols*…Carl Jung…' That imperious brow quirked again.

Sorcha was unaware of the plane touching down, announcing their arrival in New York.

'Yes,' she said tightly, holding out a hand for the book.

He gave it back after a long moment, making sure that their fingers brushed, and drawled, 'I have to admit I'm more a fan of his old adversary, Freud.'

Her fingers burned. The book was hers again. She held it to her chest and said waspishly, 'Now, why doesn't that surprise me?'

'Tell me,' he said equably, which should have had alarm bells ringing in her head, 'would this have anything to do with what Val was talking about the other night?'

She looked at him open-mouthed. And promptly shut it again. She knew if she didn't tell him he'd only ask Val. And if she didn't tell him she risked turning it into something bigger, more…

She sighed inwardly, then outwardly shrugged. She *hated* having to tell him. 'I recently graduated from NYU. I got a degree in psychology.'

He said nothing for a long moment, those eyes assessing, making her nervous. 'Val said you got a first?'

She nodded, amazed at his memory.

'Well done.'

Completely nonplussed, trying to think about what this could reveal, Sorcha just muttered something unintelligible. Too much was happening. Too much of herself was being revealed, and she felt very, very exposed. She did not want him knowing anything about her, and now he knew about the outreach centre, her degree, her fear of flying, *her attraction*...what next?

The hubbub and chatter that surrounded them as people got out of seats and collected bags gave Sorcha an excuse to get away. And she did, with barely disguised panic.

The next evening Sorcha stood huddled against the wind in her parka jacket on the top of the Empire State Building. This was where they were working for the night. The observation deck was theirs till six in the morning. These were the only shots they had to do in New York.

'So, where's Mr Tall, Dark and Gorgeous tonight?'

Sorcha felt a defensive retort about to spring from her lips and bit it back. Dominic was not the person she should allow to wind her up. So she shrugged nonchalantly, as though she didn't care, and said, 'I have no idea. Why are you so worried anyway?'

Dominic's face contorted into an ugly scowl. 'Because whenever he's around I feel like he's watching me, waiting for me to make some kind of false move.'

Sorcha had to bite back a wry smile. She didn't blame Dominic. Romain did have that ability, and she was glad that it wasn't just her on the receiving end. And, as brilliant a photographer as Dominic was, there was the element of a loose cannon about him.

The truth was, she'd been wondering the same thing herself, her senses on high alert. It *was* odd that he wasn't here, especially as tonight was the first time the other model was involved—her counterpart, her lover. This was where they were to meet for the first time, and she would have imagined that with Romain's apparent love of control he'd be watching Zane like a hawk to make sure he performed.

Sorcha knew Zane well. He was one of the most recognisable male models in the world, and had just broken out to act in a movie. He was a nice guy, easy to get on with. She heard a kerfuffle in the corner. Dominic was having a mini-tantrum about something. She could hear snatches of heated conversation, and he had a mobile clamped to his ear.

'You need to come up here now, because Claire is saying she needs approval for Zane's costume…and if we don't start shooting in the next half hour we're going to jeopardise Simon getting his dawn shots…'

Sorcha's heart started to thump. Silly. It mightn't even be him. Since he was now back in New York, she didn't doubt that he'd have made plans to take some current mistress out to dinner. Wasn't that exactly how men like Romain operated? Ruthless and controlling in business, the quintessential playboy socially—a string of women around the world.

Sorcha couldn't kid herself and think that what had happened between them had meant anything more than a bit of diverting fun for him, and that was why it couldn't happen again. He'd been playing with her—a game of showing her that he was in control.

But some minutes later, as Lucy was touching up her make-up, she saw the observation deck doors open and Romain walk out. The New York night was chilly, and he wore a long black coat that made him look impossibly tall and dark. She hadn't seen him all day and butterflies erupted in her stomach.

He focused on Dominic and Zane and went straight to them. Consulted with Claire. And then, with the issue apparently resolved, and a curt, 'Don't disturb me again unless it's *really* urgent,' he walked back out, not looking her way even momentarily.

It felt like a slap in the face—which was ridiculous when it wasn't even directed at her. She saw the lift doors close, concealing him from view. It was obvious he hadn't appreciated Dominic's autocratic demand at all.

'*He* didn't look happy to be taken away from his date!'

Sorcha looked at Lucy, and ice invaded her veins. 'What?'

Lucy shrugged. 'Well, that's where I bet he was… Why would he want to supervise us up here when he could be taking some beautiful woman out to dinner?' Lucy sighed dreamily.

Sorcha longed to be the gossiping kind just once, so she could ask her if what she'd said was based on fact. But she wasn't, so she didn't. And for the whole night, when Romain didn't reappear, Sorcha couldn't stop imagining him looking into sultry blue, or brown, or green eyes, telling her—*whoever*—that next time they wouldn't be interrupted, with all the passionate conviction he'd used with her, and which she stupidly, treacherously, couldn't get out of her head...

CHAPTER NINE

THE following night they were heading off to India. The next leg of the journey. Sorcha made sure to be one of the first on the plane this time, and chose one of the single seats. She wasn't in the mood to talk to anyone. Last night had made her feel out of control…she'd found herself missing him! As though the set had become a more sinister place without him. Everything had seemed lacklustre… They were barely days into the job and this man was winding her around his little finger with little more than his magnetic presence and one kiss. The thought of which made her squirm in her seat.

She'd tried to see Katie for lunch earlier, but it hadn't worked out with timing. Romain was insisting that they all stay in the same hotels along the way, in order to bond, so she hadn't seen her friend once. And she missed Katie's practical, down-to-earth maternal advice. Although maybe it was just as well that they hadn't met, as when she'd told Katie about taking the job her friend had seemed to think that it was a good thing. She'd probably have encouraged her to jump into bed with Romain, and that was the kind of advice that Sorcha did *not* want to hear.

She plucked her eye mask out of her bag and put it on. At least this way she wouldn't even see if he got on the plane. Because she didn't care. *Liar.* She ignored the mocking voice. And then…as if to mock her further…her heart quickened and she felt herself tremble slightly. The hairs stood up on the back of her neck when an all too familiar scent teased her nostrils. He was *here*. And she knew it without even seeing him arrive. Sorcha knew without a doubt that she was in deep trouble.

Their shooting location in India was the beautiful City of Lakes—Udaipur. It was called the most romantic city in Rajasthan, and Sorcha had to agree, taking everything in the following day as they went by boat from the shore to the Lake Palace. It rose like an eye-wateringly majestic white dream from some Arabian Nights fantasy in the middle of Lake Pichola. She loved the arid heat, the hazy blue sky and the myriad colours everywhere—some so bright that it almost hurt to look at them.

Romain sat beside her on the small seat of the boat, his thigh disturbingly close to hers. In long khaki combat shorts, much like hers, he was managing to look all at once casual and devastatingly attractive. His dark T-shirt clung to hard, defined pectoral muscles that were a wicked enticement to touch and feel. She swallowed.

She'd managed to avoid him on the plane by sleeping most of the journey, and then all the way to the plush, opulent hotel they were staying in on the shores of the lake. But for now she couldn't. She and Romain were in one boat, Simon and Dominic in another. The four were on their way to the Lake Palace to do a recce for tomorrow's shoot. The rest of the crew had the day off, to recover, get over jet lag, and they would too—once this was over.

But she couldn't stop sneaking a furtive glance. Against the backdrop of the ancient Indian buildings he looked like some regal god. And for some reason she felt compelled to speak, her mouth working independently of her brain—because what came out was *not* what she wanted to say at all.

'You were busy in New York.'

She could see his brows pull together and cursed herself. What on earth was wrong with her?

'Is that a question or a statement?' He didn't wait for her answer. 'Actually, yes, I *was* busy. I'm working on a few projects at the same time, and I knew New York would be the last place I'd have any time to spend on them... Tell me, Sorcha, did you miss me?'

She wanted to snort disdainfully, wanted to laugh. Wanted to say something cutting. She opened her mouth, but at that moment all she could see was his eyes. They were luminous in the hazy sunlight, glittering a fierce grey with something so...provocative in their depths that she couldn't say a word. She wondered with awful futility how he had this power to hold her in such a spell…to make her think of things she'd never considered before.

She was helpless, lost in that look. She wanted to blurt out how she'd been tortured with pictures of him on date after date…even though she knew in reality it had only been one night.

'I worked late that night, and then I had to take Maud out to dinner. I missed *you*.'

She couldn't breathe as something awfully exultant moved through her. How was it that he could read her mind? To her utter horror she heard her voice come out shakily, forming words she'd had no intention of saying. 'It didn't seem like that on the Empire State Building.'

A flash of something intense crossed his face, distracting her from her monumental gaffe, and then, as if she'd imagined it, he took her hand, lifting it, bringing her palm to his mouth, where he pressed a kiss to the heated middle. Her fingers curled instinctively, as if to hold the kiss, and all rational thought fled.

'I told you that next time we wouldn't be interrupted, and I meant it.'

Sorcha felt her insides quiver, the blood thicken in her veins. How did he know just what to say to make her forget everything he stood for? Everything he represented to her?

The launch arrived at the Lake Palace, and as it gently hit the small jetty wall Sorcha seemed to come to her senses. But still felt cocooned in some sort of dreamlike haze. Simon and Dominic stood waiting for them. Sorcha clambered off the boat and followed the men around. The breathtaking scenery distracted her momentarily from her churning thoughts and emotions. She gazed in wonder at the beauty of the palace, which had once been built for royalty but was now a five-star hotel.

Finished with discussing the main schedule of shots with the other men, Romain turned to look for Sorcha. She'd disappeared. He walked over to the edge of the terrace, where a complicated lattice design in marble formed a wall. And there she was, just on the level below, down a few steps. He felt that annoyingly familiar punch to the gut. With her hair free, in tousled waves down her back, she stood on the terrace below talking to one of the hotel staff. He was pointing something out to her on a carving, and she was bending down, putting on her glasses to take a closer look.

He knew she wouldn't be faking an interest. And when she turned to look up and smile widely at the man he jealously felt bowled over by her natural beauty. She was dressed simply in shorts, which showed a smooth length of pale, slim leg, and a plain white T-shirt which clung to her breasts far too provocatively for his liking. He vowed to take her, and soon. He couldn't wait much longer, and the sooner he burned himself free of this desire, the sooner he could get back to normal.

Because, as much as he relished the feeling of

boredom being gone, he also conversely wanted it back. In these uncharted waters of insatiable desire he felt rudderless. He wasn't used to a woman making him feel like this, and the only other time that had happened he'd been too young to know how to deal with it, or the consequences. Not so any more. This time he was equipped. He would take her and then move on to someone more suitable, *safer*. This was just a temporary madness.

At that moment, as if Sorcha sensed him watching, she turned and looked up. The smile slid from her face and was replaced with a flare in her eyes. Her mouth opened slightly. She wanted him too. He knew it like an immutable truth that stirred in his blood. Though he knew she'd deny it again if he pushed her.

And that was why he found himself tugging her back from getting on the boat as they watched Simon and Dominic go off ahead of them. Now they were alone. No crew around.

Sorcha looked up into Romain's expressionless face. She was very aware of the fact that they were now alone. On a stunningly beautiful idyllic white marbled palace island. Dominic and Simon's boat was chugging away in the distance. Their boatman was looking at them expectantly.

'Have lunch with me here.'

Sorcha's immediate and first reaction was to shake her head and say no. A strong suspicion assailed her, making her quite sure that he was only asking so he could keep her close, could make sure she stayed out of trouble. Romain saw her hesitation. He smiled, and it looked dangerous and far too seductive.

'Don't worry—I won't ravish you. And you have to eat, don't you?'

She opened her mouth, and to her utter horror and chagrin her stomach made a sound like water going down a very big, echoing drain. She promptly shut her mouth and blushed.

'That settles it.' He took her arm and shepherded her back up the steps and into the main open-air foyer of the hotel.

The feeling of unreality lingered as they were shown to a secluded table in the corner of the magnificent restaurant. There were no walls, only columns, open to the warm air, the hazy blue of the sky and the lapping waters of the lake, intricately carved with complicated mosaics which were echoed in the roof above. It was truly the most breathtaking place Sorcha had ever been in her life.

A waiter materialised and she heard Romain order a bottle of champagne. She stopped him with a brief, light touch on his hand. He looked at her quizzically.

'I'm sorry but do you mind if we don't have champagne? It's just that it gives me a headache…'

She sent a small, hesitant smile to the waiter and then back to Romain, who felt slightly winded.

'If you don't mind…what I'd actually really like is a beer.'

He lifted a brow and felt totally nonplussed. It had

been pure reflex to order champagne—his first step in any seduction. And she wanted *beer*? He couldn't remember the last time he'd even drunk a beer, and yet in that instant it seemed to him to be the most desirable drink in the world.

He nodded to the waiter. 'Two beers, please.'

Sorcha felt embarrassed as the waiter scurried away. 'Oh, you don't have to have one just because of me... That is,' she qualified, feeling awkward, 'you don't exactly look like a beer drinking man.'

He sat back. His face was all lean angles, making him look austere.

'Tell me, what *do* I look like?'

Like a man who knows how to make love to a woman...

Sorcha's insides liquefied, and she couldn't believe how a bubble of sensuality seemed to have enveloped them.

She had to control herself with effort. 'You look like a vintage champagne type. Or a thousand-euro-a-bottle of wine type.'

He had actually paid that much and more for wine in the past, and it seemed almost crass now. 'Forgive me. I should have consulted with you before ordering. Though, after seeing you put away half a glass of champagne in one go in New York, I was under the impression that you liked it.'

Sorcha had the grace to smile. 'I actually hate the stuff. I wouldn't have had a glass at all, only for Katie giving me one. Maud likes us to look like we're having a good time at events like that…drinking champagne promotes the stereotype.'

'And you *weren't* having a good time?' he asked easily.

The beers arrived. Romain held his bottle up and Sorcha clinked hers to his. Without breaking eye contact, they both took a long swallow.

Romain closed his eyes for a second. 'I'd forgotten how good it tastes—especially in this climate…' He opened them again, catching Sorcha looking at him with glittering big blue eyes. His body tightened. 'Go on, you were going to tell me why you weren't having a good time…'

She was? She had to be careful. To her consternation, she was finding that he was all too easy to talk to. It would be very easy to let something slip out that she wasn't ready to talk about.

She shrugged minutely. 'Well, you saw what it was like. A room full of movers and shakers. We were there primarily as adornments. People look at us and think: Models—ergo stupid. It's all about seeing and being seen.'

She looked out to the lake. 'In the early days it was all fabulously exciting to be in the same room as the Mayor of New York, or the biggest, newest film star, but really…your illusions get stripped away pretty quickly. Coming from somewhere like Ireland, I think I have a pretty good inbuilt detector for anyone who isn't genuine. And about one per cent of that crowd *are* genuine…'

What she said brought back a niggling sense of *déjà vu*, but before he could dwell on it, pin it down, the waiter returned and took their order. Romain ordered more beers, and Sorcha was surprised to see they'd already been talking for some time. Her eyes took in his relaxed stance, his T-shirt straining across the muscles of his chest. She remembered seeing him emerge from the sea in Ireland. He smiled and she couldn't breathe. The brown column of his throat looked all too touchable.

It felt as if a silken cord of intimacy was wrapping itself around Sorcha.

She spoke to fill the silence which seemed far too heavy and potent for her, seizing on the first thing that came into her head.

'I was here before…' She answered his questioning look, 'On a backpacking trip with my friend Katie, when we were twenty-one. We'd been on a shoot in Delhi, and decided to do a little travelling before going home. We stayed at a tiny hostel just across the water there somewhere. We used to sit in our window, drinking beers. We'd dream about being over here, having a sumptuous meal, fine wine…'

She couldn't stop a sudden giggle from rising, and Romain watched her. She didn't realise how infectious her grin was. She knew part of it was a slightly hysterical reaction to being here in the first place, sharing such an intimate space with this man. At how fast things were moving, changing…

'I'm sorry—it's just that if Katie could see me now, she'd be so horrified...' The giggle crept higher, and Sorcha bit her lip to stop it erupting. But when she saw a twitch on Romain's mouth she couldn't help it spilling out.

'The fact that I'm here in shorts and a T-shirt, fulfilling our fantasy...and drinking *beer*...' A tear escaped from her eye and she had to wipe it away, laughing in earnest now. 'She'd *kill* me!'

A grin broke out on Romain's face, and that sobered her up quicker than anything—the sheer masculine perfection of his features.

Her giggles died away with a little hiccup. 'Sorry...it's just if you'd seen the place we were staying... If Katie was here, she'd be dignity personified...not like me, swilling beer and corrupting your fine palate. Maybe you should have brought her,' she said lightly, too lightly.

Romain shook his head. 'I'm not interested in her.'

Sorcha's heart pounded uncomfortably into the silence.

'Tell me,' he asked, 'you're good friends?'

Sorcha nodded emphatically. This was easy. 'The best. She's been there for me since—' She broke off, stopping her runaway mouth, and finished, 'Since for ever. We've known each other since we were ten...and got discovered at the same time by a scout from Dublin when we were fifteen.'

At that moment their food was delivered. With relief at finding his intense focus off her for a moment, Sorcha tucked into the food, suddenly ravenous. They shared starters of traditional samosas and spring rolls wrapped Vietnamese-style in rice paper. Then Sorcha had ordered a main dish of steamed sea bass, while Romain had opted for a dish unique to the region, *khad khargosh*—wild hare.

When his meal was placed in front of him, and he saw Sorcha wrinkle her nose slightly, he asked, with a quirk to his mouth, 'You don't approve?'

Horrified to be caught like that, she said quickly, 'Oh, no. It's just the thought of the poor little hare…sorry.'

He speared a morsel and ate it, completely unperturbed. 'But you're not a vegetarian. You ordered steak that day in Dublin.'

When she'd fled the restaurant like a bolshy teenager…

She looked slightly shame faced and put her fork down for a moment, lifting her eyes to his. All he could see was their luminosity. Her colouring was exotic against this backdrop.

'I don't normally run out like that.'

He inclined his head slightly in acknowledgement. And felt surprised. He was used to women being petulant, yet that day he knew she hadn't been. Her speedy exit had come from something much deeper. He'd touched on a raw nerve, and he remembered that they'd been talking about her project—the outreach centre. What he'd said then seemed to him to be unbelievably insensitive now. He'd still been labouring under his misapprehension, not believing that she might be different, *reformed*.

And was she?

Introspection kept him quiet. He was thinking about how professional she was. So far she'd been nothing but pleasant, polite, helpful, quiet…not a hint of divadom at all. All qualities his aunt had professed her to have *again* when he'd taken her for dinner. A dinner in which he'd had to focus just to get Sorcha out of his head. That was why he'd largely ignored her when Dominic had called him up to the set in New York. He'd known that seeing her would have the potential to scramble his brain. And he was not comfortable with that at all. He'd known her for less than three weeks, and hadn't even slept with her…*yet*.

With the last succulent morsel of sea bass dissolving on her tongue, Sorcha sat back and dabbed her napkin to her mouth. 'That was…amazing.'

Romain sat back too. 'Yes. And if you want you can tell Kate you had champagne…the works…I'll back up your story.'

Sorcha grinned and held up her bottle of beer to gently clink it with his in collusion. It was only when she took a swallow and saw some kind of triumphant gleam in his eye that her blood ran cold. What was he doing? Acting as if she and he might be in a situation in the future where they would create this little *in joke* to share with Katie…or whoever? Almost as if they were a couple.

And what the hell was *she* doing? This man was

the enemy…and yet at this lunch it felt as if he was anything but. She felt shivery and trembly inside. This man was playing with her, that was all.

The plates were cleared away, a clean table lay between them. And then her fears were compounded.

He leant forward, two elbows on the table. Intent. 'I owe you an apology.'

Sorcha tensed slightly. 'You do?'

He nodded. 'That day in Dublin, what I said about your outreach centre, it was unforgivable. I had no right to judge something you've been working on— no right to judge your motivations for doing something like that.'

Sorcha floundered. This Romain was way, way more dangerous to deal with than the autocratic, overbearing Romain.

'Well, thank you.'

Now please drop it, she begged silently.

'Would you tell me about it?'

Sorcha fought against closing her eyes. Her plea had gone spectacularly unanswered. She thought quickly. What harm could it do to tell him just a little? Surely it wouldn't really give away anything? She took a deep breath.

Romain had seen the conflict cross her face, the shadows in her eyes again, the effort it was taking for her to open up to him at all. It made him feel a whole host of conflicting emotions, not least the desire to ask himself, *what does she have to hide?*

Sorcha looked out to the lake, and when she

looked back to Romain her eyes were guarded. 'When my father died… Well, we were very close.'

Romain gave a tiny nod of his head, encouraging her to go on. She looked at him steadily, and he was aware at that moment of something powerful passing between them.

'He was my best friend, my confidante.' She shrugged lightly and looked down for a second. 'I was the ultimate daddy's girl. He used to happily tell everyone that he was wrapped around my finger… he'd bring me to his office…everywhere. He died suddenly. No warning—nothing. I got the call from my mum while I was at school. My older brother was away with his family…' She shrugged again, and this time it was jerky, as though she was fighting to keep the emotion down.

'I kind of went off the rails a bit. I left school that summer, and Katie and I had both been offered work in London. Unfortunately I got involved with a crowd of less than savoury characters, and a guy called Christian. I was still very angry about my father's death, and hadn't really dealt with it. At that age there's not a lot of emotional support unless you get it at home…'

Romain stayed very still and quiet, his eyes holding hers, and when she looked at him they seemed to her to be like beacons. Crazy…but very, very seductive. She kept talking.

'I guess that's where the desire came from to do…*something*. For years I've always thought that if there had been some place…somewhere to go…that had offered impartial, confidential advice and support, I might have gone. And I might not have…' She didn't finish, and couldn't look at him any more.

Romain reached across the table and took her hand, covering it with his warmth. Dark against pale. She only realised then that she was shaking.

'Was Dominic a part of that crowd?'

She looked at him. 'How…?'

'He mentioned something at the start about knowing you from years ago. I put two and two together.'

She nodded. 'Christian was his friend.'

'Was Christian your lover?' he asked sharply.

Her sense of danger skyrocketed.

How can I say I'm not sure…? Sorcha thought crazily to herself. She gave a brief, abrupt shake of the head. 'No. I had a crush…it was all quite innocent…'

He seemed satisfied with that, and Sorcha prayed he'd move away from such dangerous waters.

'Is that why you did the psychology degree? So you could work at the centre?' He shook his own head. 'I only realised when you told me about it that you wouldn't have had time to come home for any real length of time…again, I'm sorry Sorcha…'

CHAPTER TEN

SORCHA struggled to stay calm, but she felt like she wanted to get up and run—hide, go away. With every word he was saying he was getting closer, digging deeper, and soon he'd reach the very centre of everything, the place were her desire threatened to bubble out of control.

She pulled her hand back and racked her brain for some way to take the intense spotlight off her.

'And what about you? What are your secrets, Romain?' Her voice felt very brittle, like her control. 'How come you're not married?'

Where had *that* come from?

Romain sat back. At least she'd had the desired effect. His eyes narrowed on hers.

'I was engaged once, actually…'

'You were?' Sorcha's treacherous heart fell.

He nodded briefly, curtly. 'Yes. A long time ago. I was eighteen.' His mouth twisted cynically. 'She was my first true love. But one day I walked into her bedroom and caught her in bed with my older half-brother.'

The words were said without a hint of emotion, but Sorcha could intuit the pain. God only knew, she'd become so adept at hiding her own innermost emotions that she could see it a mile away in someone else. But she knew he wouldn't welcome sympathy.

One big shoulder shrugged with apparent insouciance. 'She'd found out that he stood to inherit the title of Duc. While I too have inherited a title, it's that of mere Comte. He was older, richer, more experienced—and he also stood to inherit the family château.'

He felt familiar satisfaction rush through him when he thought of how he'd bought back that château just a couple of years before. His brother had come to him, begging for aid. And yet, even though it had been a moment he'd waited for a long time, the satisfaction, while still there, hadn't tasted as sweet as he'd thought it would. He'd somewhere along the way lost that all-consuming desire to get back at the brother who had made his life a complete misery from when he was a small child.

'I'm sorry…I didn't mean to bring up something so—'

Before she could say *painful*, and put a word to his feelings, Romain laughed harshly. 'It was a long time ago. She was dead to me a long time ago, and since then—' he made a very Gallic facial expression '—I haven't had the inclination to repeat the experience.'

His face and demeanour said it all to Sorcha. He'd tarred every woman since then with the same brush.

His treatment of her said it all too. His obvious ruth-lessness in his desire to get her into bed, despite his initial misgivings, which were conveniently dropping away. Which she was allowing him, *helping* him to shed. God, did she want him so badly that she was contemplating letting someone so jaded take her in the most intimate way?

She couldn't read his expression. A tense silence surrounded them and then, as if a switch had been flicked on, he smiled. Jekyll and Hyde. Sorcha shivered.

'I think we've had enough questions and answers—yes?'

She nodded mutely.

'Let's have some dessert…' And he called over the waiter.

Within minutes, he was fast weaving her headlong into the tapestry of desire again, making her forget all her misgivings.

On the boat on their way back to the hotel, the mood was considerably lighter. He made her laugh uncontrollably with funny stories about various fashion designers and their prima donna behaviour. And then she remembered something he had said earlier. 'So you're a count? What does that make you—Monsieur le Comte de Valois?'

He looked at her sharply. He hadn't mistaken the teasing in her tone, even if her face was serious.

He nodded. 'I never use it though. It seems a bit outdated these days.'

'Oh, I don't know.' Sorcha slid him a mischievous glance. 'A count with, I assume, at least one château?' she asked, looking to him for confirmation. He nodded again. 'Well, that's quite the package. In that case I should have curtsied when we met…'

Now she was definitely laughing at him. He couldn't believe it. For a second he felt all the righteous anger and pride of his forebears, and then at the next moment, seeing her mouth twitch helplessly, he had to give in.

'How refreshing—a woman who isn't dropping at my feet with the mention of a title and a château.'

Again he had that split second sensation of thinking, *she's playing me…*

She looked at him from under long black lashes. There was no make-up on her slightly freckled face, and she was so beautiful that his chest ached. But even as he looked he saw something come into her eyes, and she drew back, inwards.

They made the rest of the trip in silence. He could feel Sorcha becoming more and more tense beside him. On disembarking the boat she said a quick brusque thank you and didn't meet his eye, then she fled.

Romain watched her go, a small predatory smile playing around his hard mouth.

A little later, after a shower, Sorcha gave up trying to have a siesta—too jittery and on edge after that lunch. She felt overloaded with sensations and desires and feelings that confused her. One in particular being that she had to admit to herself that she *liked* him. Really liked him. As for what he did to her body…just thinking about that made her heat up.

She decided to take a walk in the nearby streets to try and calm down.

She ducked into an ornate Hindu temple, feeling for a moment as if she were being followed, and cursed her imagination. Inside, all the different deities were painted in a profusion of bright colours. Little children danced around her, asking for 'school pens', and gave her incense to light. She took some pictures. Those moments, and as she walked through markets, bought herself some clothes, gave her some sense of equilibrium back.

The streets were heaving with humanity, sacred cows and eye-wateringly strong smells. She dodged the rickshaws that held beautiful and mysterious sari-clad women and thought that she was mad to be even *thinking* about anything to do with Romain de Valois. She was no match for him. He just didn't realise it yet.

Returning to the hotel, she was relieved not to have bumped into anyone, but in the corridor on the way back to her room she heard a hissed, 'Sorcha!'

It was Lucy, in the room next to hers. 'Are you OK?'

Lucy looked up and down the corridor and gestured for Sorcha to come in.

She groaned inwardly. She really didn't want to get all girly and chat. But when she got to the door Lucy pulled her inside, shutting the door after her.

'Lucy, I'm really tired—'

'I have something you might be interested in.'

The hair stood up on the back of Sorcha's neck. The younger girl held out a small paper packet full of white powder. Sorcha's stomach fell. She'd encountered this over the years—people mistakenly believing what they might have heard…

'Look, Lucy, I'm really not interested in that stuff. And you shouldn't go waving it around.'

Lucy laughed. 'Oh, don't be such a square. Come on—what's the harm?'

Something hard settled in Sorcha's chest. She made a split-second decision, and behind it was the urge to protect. She grabbed the paper out of Lucy's hand, folding it up carefully.

'Hey—' The girl's face was a picture of surprise and panic.

Sorcha quickly stuck it in the back pocket of her shorts and folded her arms.

'Lucy, how old are you?'

'Twenty-one.'

She looked a little shame-faced, and Sorcha was relieved to see that it didn't look as if she'd taken any of the drug yet. She gentled her tone.

'Look, if anyone else had caught you with this…like Romain…you'd be going home on the next plane. And you'd probably never get work again. Not to mention we're in India. Do you have any idea what the police here would do if you were caught?'

She saw Lucy pale visibly. Sorcha grimaced inwardly. No doubt Dominic had her under his thumb. And she didn't want to scare her.

'I don't care where you got it, because I know who probably gave it to you—' The other girl went red and started to bluster. Sorcha just held up a hand. 'Believe me, I know Dominic from a long time ago, so don't feel you have to protect him. And, Lucy, if you'll take some advice from me, the next time someone offers you drugs don't be a fool and take them. The person you offer to share them with might not be so understanding or get rid of it for you…'

Sorcha left and went back to her own room next door. It felt as if the white powder was burning a hole in her pocket. She dropped her shopping bag and went straight to her bathroom. She was about to flush it down the loo, when a knock came on her door. Panicking slightly, she stuffed it again into her back pocket.

She opened the door and felt immediately dizzy. Romain stood there, larger than life. And then, without so much as a by-your-leave, he sauntered in as if he owned the place. Sorcha gripped the door handle, loath to shut the door. *What was he doing here? He had to leave!* She could feel herself pale. She could feel the packet, and it suddenly weighed a ton. A cold sweat broke out on her brow. Of all the times!

'Can…can I help you?' she asked, and her voice sounded strained to her ears.

He leant back against the door that opened out onto her patio. His eyes narrowed on her face and Sorcha felt herself flush guiltily. *What was he doing here?*

'Shut the door,' he said quietly.

Sorcha's mind raced even as she did as he asked, not thinking to question it. Could he have seen anything? Overheard anything? He couldn't have... This had to be unrelated. Because if it wasn't... Her blood ran cold.

The door shut behind her, and Romain called softly from across the room. 'Come here.'

Feeling more and more like Alice in Wonderland, slipping down a hole, Sorcha haltingly moved forward. If she could just get into the bathroom—

'You don't need to look like you're about to go to your own funeral,' he drawled, 'It'll be nice, I promise...'

Sorcha looked at him then, and stopped by the bed. He'd cut through the turmoil in her brain even as her insides clawed with guilt. Nice? She shook her head as if that might try and clear it. 'I'm sorry...look... what do you want?'

He pushed himself off the door and strolled towards her with dangerous intent in his eye. Too late, Sorcha realised what his intention was only when he came so close that she couldn't breathe.

'I told you that next time we wouldn't be inter-rupted...'

He couldn't mean...

'I want *you*.'

He did. Within a cataclysmic split second Sorcha's world was reduced to Romain pulling her into his arms, chest to chest, and before she could say *stop*, or *go*, or even take a breath, his mouth was stealing every bit of sanity from her.

The rush of sensation and reaction made her forget everything. With shocking ease, her whole being melted into his.

The matter of fact way he'd just come in…the intent in his eyes that reached out to wrap her in a haze of desire…it scrambled her brain so much that all she was aware of was the need to have him kiss her again, to feel his arms around her. That last kiss was seared onto her memory, and now she was coming back to life in his arms.

His mouth moved over hers with insistent mastery. A flame of white-hot desire was racing along every one of Sorcha's veins, and when her mouth opened on a little sigh, and his tongue made contact with hers, her hands reached out and tightened on his shoulders to stop herself from falling at his feet.

Sorcha's two arms twined up around his neck. She stood on tiptoe, couldn't stop the hitched indrawn breath against his mouth when she felt his hand on her back, reaching under her T-shirt to stroke up over the silky skin, moulding the outline of the curve of her waist. An aching wanting grew at the apex of her thighs, and when Sorcha innocently moved her hips, felt his arousal press insistently against her, her heart beat so fast she thought it would burst from her chest.

His arms around her felt so good, so strong, and when one hand moved down to cup her bottom through her shorts, moving her even closer, she couldn't help a little mewl of acquiescence. His hand on her bottom sought to get even closer. She felt him slide it into her pocket—

Sorcha's whole body went rigid in a second. As if ice had just been poured through every artery. His hand was *right there*.

She pulled back and looked up into his face. She couldn't help the look of shock she knew must be there. At another time his reaction might have been almost comical.

He looked surprised at first. Then a small frown appeared and, with deadly, awful inevitability, his fingers closed around the small paper packet and she felt him pull it free from her back pocket. His arms slackened, and all the heat and insanity disappeared as he let her go.

Romain stepped back and a chasm opened up, like an arctic wind blowing between them. Sorcha's eyes closed, her hands were dead weights by her side. She didn't think she was even breathing. The situation was so horrifically awful and unfair she couldn't take in the magnitude of what it meant.

His voice was so cold when it came that it made her flinch.

'Open your eyes.'

She opened them, and could feel the colour drain from her face again. She was freezing.

He held the folded-up paper which had opened slightly, revealing the white powder between his forefinger and thumb, a look of complete and utter disgust on his face—much the same as hers had been only short moments before. Moments which now felt like years.

'I...' Her voice felt scratchy and her lips and mouth still tingled.

'There is not one thing you can say. Not. One. Thing.'

Sorcha's mouth shut. The total and utter immediate condemnation on his face shocked her. He hadn't even a shred of doubt in his mind...and why would he? But it hurt. She bit the inside of her lip so hard she could feel blood. She wrapped her arms around her waist and felt shock set in, felt the shaking starting up, that awful dropping of her stomach—even though she hadn't even done anything wrong!

But one thing she did know, and it was very clear. She could not subject Lucy to this man's wrath. She was just a young girl, starting out in her career. And Sorcha knew she'd look even worse in Romain's eyes if she tried to blame someone else younger, more inexperienced.

Having made the decision to take the blame, or at least protect Lucy, Sorcha felt a kind of calmness wash over her. After all, what did she really have to lose? Wasn't this what he had expected all along?

The shaking subsided.

Romain saw her chin tilt up minutely, her shoulders straighten. A light of defiance come into her eyes. And as the awful, betraying disappointment rushed through him he felt himself get cold and hard inside. *Fool, fool, fool.* And yet even now, in the midst of this, he was taking in her huge blue eyes, the delicate pale column of her throat, the way her breasts pushing at the thin fabric of her T-shirt made him think of the way they had just pushed against his chest. And, much to his abject horror, his body reacted to that image, that thought.

He moved towards her, and all Sorcha's paltry bravado disappeared. He took her arm in a harsh grip and half-dragged, half-walked her over to the bathroom.

He was curt and harsh. 'You know what to do.'

He thrust the folded-up parcel at her as if it was contaminating him, and Sorcha felt like crying, laughing and screaming all at the same time. What would he say if she told him that this was exactly what she had been about to do before being interrupted?

With shaking hands she emptied it into the toilet, flushing the offending drug away. The sound was magnified unbearably in the tense atmosphere. With legs shaking so much that she'd fall if she didn't sit, she sank back onto the side of the bath. She looked at the ground. She had to try something.

'Romain—'

'I don't want to hear it.'

She looked up, her eyes huge, beseeching, and quailed at the coldness she saw in his face. It was nothing like she'd ever experienced.

She tried again. 'It's not what you—'

He laughed harshly, arms crossed against his chest. Arms that had just now held her so tight she'd never wanted him to let her go. She ached inside.

'*Think?* That's original. No wonder you were in such a hurry after lunch. Tell me…' he said, and he relaxed back against the sink, one hip propped up. But the lines of his body screamed anything *but* relaxed. 'Was the whole purpose of your little walk just now to get drugs? Is that why you were so eager to get away? Because you needed a fix? Did you have someone lined up before we even got here? I'm interested to know how this would work. Do you call ahead. Or is it—'

'Stop it!' Her hands gripped the edge of the bath as she tried to make sense of what he was saying, the barrage of questions. 'I… How do you…?'

'How do I know you took a walk?' he asked. 'Because I was taking a walk myself, and saw you go into the temple.'

His mouth twisted as he remembered following her. Being captivated by her.

He looked unbearably harsh. 'Charming picture. Playing with the kids…taking photos…lighting incense.' He shook his head. '*Dieu*…what a fool I am. You were on your way to pick up your stash. I actually thought—'

He cut himself off. His eyes were so glacial that Sorcha felt as if a layer of her skin was being peeled off slowly. But she couldn't take her eyes from his.

'I lost you, though…after the market where you bought that *salwaar kameez*. That's obviously when you went off to find your little…contact.'

She shook her head miserably and stood, legs still shaking.

'I promise you…it's not what you think.'

'Promise me? That's rich.' He stood upright and towered over her in the small space. 'To think that in Dublin when you asked if I would believe you'd never touched drugs I actually thought about it…considered it…I would have believed it if I'd heard nothing but your chain of lies today. But only a mere hour after telling me breathlessly about the outreach centre, how important it is, you're—'

A look flashed across his face, and as if he'd said too much he cursed in French and strode back out into the bedroom.

Sorcha followed him, stood at the door of the bathroom. He had his back to her, looking out of the patio doors. She didn't know where to start, what to say. She could see exactly how he would construe events…words…and could only watch his taut, unrelenting back helplessly. And even in the midst of this the memory of how it had felt… He turned and fixed her with those cold eyes, and immediately her skin flushed guiltily. As if he could see her shameful thoughts.

'What are you going to do?' she asked bravely, and steeled herself.

He looked at her for a long moment. She could almost see the cogs whirring in that sharp brain. And then, as if having come to a decision, he strolled nonchalantly towards her. His face was unbearably cold, but the look in his eyes was full of desirous intent. His demeanour spelt absolute danger. Sorcha instinctively grabbed onto the wall beside her as he came close. She looked up helplessly. Ensnared.

And suddenly she thought of something.

Without passing it through the filter in her brain, she found herself blurting out, 'Look, I know why you're reacting like this. I know what happened with your mother...'

CHAPTER ELEVEN

HE STOPPED dead in front of her, and immediately she knew she'd made one of the biggest errors of her life. He froze. His face became a mask of non-reaction, his eyes glittering jewel-hard shards of icy grey. He spoke after what felt like aeons, and his words dripped with disdain and disgust.

'What do you know?'

It was a question but Sorcha wasn't foolish enough to open her mouth again.

'Maud told you. It can only have been her. What did she tell you?'

This person before her was someone Sorcha had never seen. Even at his most dismissive, judging…this *cold* creature hadn't existed. A thousand miles gaped between this man and the man who'd taken her for lunch, the man who had kissed her.

He moved closer, and Sorcha tried to move back but the wall was in her way. She wanted to apologise, wanted to tell him that he was scaring her.

'Did Maud tell you that my mother was addicted to opium since she was a child growing up in Vietnam?'

Sorcha, horribly mesmerized by his nearness and eyes, just shook her head.

'Did Maud tell you that she lived her whole life in a drug-fuelled haze?'

Again she shook her head, horror spreading through her. He came even closer. She could feel his body now, his chest moving up and down against hers, and to her utter self-loathing she could feel herself respond, her nipples tightening.

'Did she tell you that she only came out of it long enough to have me and my older half-brother? To make two unhappy marriages?'

Sorcha couldn't do anything. He was so close now that she could feel his breath. His head came close and a hand was cupping her jaw, angling her head up to his. *Please*, she wanted to beg. *Stop.*

'Did she tell you that at the age of seventeen I found her dead body? Bloated and almost unrecognisable from an overdose?'

An ache clogged Sorcha's throat, and her eyes stung. With his hand cupping her jaw she couldn't move her head. She opened her mouth to try and say something, to reach him, and he took advantage, driving his mouth down on hers, full of pent-up aggression and anger.

Sorcha's hand had come up to his, to try and take it away, but in her shock she left it there. His words were swirling in her head, but all she could feel was him, wrapping his arms around her again, his tongue dancing erotically with hers. He was relentless, a master of her senses, and she could do nothing but succumb even as she felt a tear trickle out from under one eyelid and down her cheek.

After a long, long moment Romain pulled back with a jerky, violent movement and looked down at her. He shook with reaction—to what he'd just revealed, to what he'd found on Sorcha's person, and most of all to the way she was making him feel. To the way she held his body in her spell. He could see wetness on her cheek, where a lone tear had left its mark, but instead of inciting concern, he welcomed the hardness that settled in every bone. She was looking up at him with those big eyes. Lips trembling, plump from his kiss. And he would have her. Even though it went against every moral principle he'd held dear. Even though he'd hate himself. Because he couldn't *not*.

'You asked what I'm going to do, Sorcha…well, this is what I'm going to do. I'm going to take your delectable body when I'm good and ready. And I'm going to sate myself with you, burn myself free of this desire I feel.'

Sorcha swallowed painfully, her head and insides in absolute chaotic turmoil. 'But…you mean… you're not going to send me home?'

He shook his head and a cruel smile touched his mouth. 'No way. At this stage that would cost me money…' He trailed a finger down her cheek and around her jaw. 'And cost me my sanity. You're going to finish the job…as my mistress…'

* * *

Long after he had left the room, with nothing more than a curt reminder to be ready to leave for the set at five in the morning, Sorcha sat on the bed in a daze. With a weird, bizarre calmness that she knew was shock, she was thinking of all the advances she'd had from men over the years.

She'd inevitably found their attentions unwelcome, jarring, and very unsexy. As a result, she was vastly inexperienced when it came to men and sex. She had an ongoing fear that somehow she was *cold*, or *frigid*. More than one man had hurled those words at her. But, any man who'd tried to touch her with any kind of intimacy had left her feeling cold. And yet Romain was making her feel anything but frigid. Even when subjecting her to his ice-cold disdain.

Why, oh why, did it have to be him? She lay back, rolled over, and curled up into a foetal position. She could never be intimate with someone who was judging her so harshly, even though she knew she couldn't blame him for this latest development. She had chosen to protect Lucy, and he'd had all the ammunition ready and lined up for just such a situation. And mentioning his mother? She squeezed her eyes shut, the pain of his words still sinking in like knives. She concentrated her breathing and forced her mind away from it, from the sympathy that still gripped her.

In turmoil, she thought of his autocratic assurance that he would make her his mistress. She knew that he wouldn't have to do much. He'd pretty much established that just by looking at her she turned to jelly and was his. It was pathetic.

She couldn't stop her mind going back… Eight years ago something had happened to her. And even to this day she wasn't sure *what*. How could she explain that to someone who was the least likely to believe her explanation of how she'd ended up in that awful spiral of events? She'd always expected that the moment she decided to let someone be totally intimate with her would be the moment she revealed herself fully. She'd never done that with anyone. Not even Katie or her brother—and they were the only people she trusted in the world.

How could she sleep with someone…with *him*… when she didn't even know for sure if she was a virgin? She grimaced painfully. She was sure on an intellectual level that she was. But on some other level, deep down, enough doubt that had been placed in her mind to question herself…and that was a torture she only wanted to share with someone gentle enough, sensitive enough to handle it. She knew well how awful it would sound if she tried to explain, as though. As though—

She couldn't even go there with herself.

She buried her face in the bed, as if to block her predicament out completely. She wasn't successful.

Sorcha moved from behind a leafy palm and stepped into the glittering white of the inner courtyard. It was dusk. A shimmering pool in the middle offered up reflections of the surrounding intricately carved walls. A bird of paradise flew through in a quicksilver flash of colour. Lotus flowers sat on the water like flowering jewels. And there, on the other side of this oasis of beauty, stood her lover, waiting for her. She walked slowly, as if in a dream, felt the silk of her long dress moving like liquid satin against her legs. She reached him. A stunning portrait of handsome perfection in a black tuxedo. He pulled her into his arms and kissed her.

Simon's voice rang out. 'That's great, Sorcha and Zane. We'll do it one more time, and then it's Dominic's turn.'

Sorcha smiled at Zane as he let her go. It was a brittle smile, and hid the aching hurt in her throat and chest. It had taken Lucy a lot longer today to do her make-up, after her sleepless night, and it hadn't been helped by the girl's monosyllabic bad mood. Sorcha couldn't feel bad as she was the one who had acted on a reflex, taken the drugs from her and decided to protect her.

She had refused to acknowledge or look to where she knew Romain stood behind a monitor, watching proceedings as they were filmed. Except just now, walking over to Zane, trying desperately to act her heart out, she'd found a lean, autocratic face coming into her mind's eye, superimposing itself onto Zane's features. And it was actually only six-thirty a.m. They were pretending it was dusk. There was a whole lot of day left to get through.

* * *

By midday, Romain was pacing like a caged tiger. Seeing Sorcha at the crack of dawn in a dress that was breathtakingly *indecent* was testing his control to the limit. Along with the fact that she hadn't acknowledged him once, and skittered away if he came near her. Right now she was seated on the corner of the set. She was a picture of contradictions that made his head swim. And the inarticulate rage from yesterday was still close under the surface.

The long, flowing silver-grey dress clung precariously to the soft swells of her breasts. A diamond clipped just under her bosom was the only feature, and the dress fell from there to the floor in a swirling symphony of silk. What had made his trousers feel tight all morning was the fact that it had an artful thigh-high slit. So when she walked one long, lithe and luscious leg peeped out in all its lissome glory.

His decision, his announcement to her that he would take her as his mistress, was making it hard for him to rein in the desire. He cursed himself again for not just taking her last night. Why had he left her alone?

Uncomfortably, he knew why. Because too much had happened, too quickly. He'd reeled with the shock of coming face to face with her duplicity, with the hard evidence…the image of that white powder still made his stomach contract. Reeled at the fact that all along she *had* been playing him, with what he'd revealed about his mother, and reeled at how, even after all this, he could *still* want her. Even more. It burned him up inside.

He couldn't take his eyes off her. With her hair piled high, exposing a long graceful neck, she looked like a teenager playing dress-up. Her shoes were off, her legs were crossed, one small bare foot peeping out from under the folds of silk. Her brow was creased over her glasses in concentration as she read her book.

Who was she trying to kid?

After lunch, Sorcha waited for them to get the next set-up ready. She was congratulating herself on having managed to avoid Romain all morning, but every time she saw where they'd had lunch the previous day, on the other side of the courtyard, she felt ill. Clammy and sweaty.

She heard Dominic call for her impatiently. He had it in for her today, and she could only imagine that Lucy must have told him what she'd done. She prayed that he wouldn't make an issue of it. She should have guessed that things wouldn't be going her way…

Hours later everyone was crabby: a mixture of the dense, heavy heat and the jet lag which some were still suffering from. Dominic had become so unbearable that Sorcha felt compelled to go over to him and say something—anything, to get him to lay off. She'd even seen Romain raise a brow at one stage, when he'd been sharp to the point of rudeness. When she confronted him he turned on her, making her blanch, and real fear struck her. It was only then that she realised they were cut off from everyone else, behind a huge plant.

He gripped her arm at the elbow, drawing her further into seclusion, and Sorcha bit back a retort.

'How *dare* you play almighty God with Lucy? It's none of your business what—'

Sorcha refused to let the fear rise, to be bullied, and she rallied back. 'It *is* my business when it's offered to me, Dominic. And what are you doing, giving her that kind of stuff anyway? She's barely out of her teens.'

He smirked, and it was ugly. 'Yet she pleasures me every night like an adult.'

Sorcha felt bile rise, and tried to wrestle her arm away—but his wiry strength was too much.

'But you know, Sorch, I'd much prefer to taste your sweetness. Christian told me all about you… how sweet you taste…'

A black hole threatened to consume Sorcha. Her deepest, darkest fear was being articulated out loud, *here*, by this odious man.

'Come on, Sorch, just a kiss…'

He pulled her into his wiry body, and she struggled in earnest now. This was a nightmare. What had possessed her to think she could reason with someone like this?

Bending away so far that it felt her back might break, she still felt hot breath on her neck. Panic gripped her. She pushed against him. 'Dominic— *no*!'

'Come on…just pretend it's lover boy…'

His mouth touched her skin. She felt teeth. A wave of dizziness washed over her, and then in an instant he was gone, pulled back so brutally that she went forward with him, and would have fallen if Romain hadn't caught her, an arm holding her steady away from Dominic.

'This is not the time or place.' His voice was so chilling that Sorcha was reminded of the previous day. 'Now, go back out there and finish the job you've been paid to do.'

Dominic just nodded, a mottled flush on his cheeks, his eyes overbright. Sorcha couldn't believe it. He was high! How had she not even noticed?

When he had gone, Romain turned Sorcha to face him. She was shaking all over. He didn't allow it to move him. He was still hard and unrelenting.

'We'll talk about this later.'

He had a hand under her arm and was leading her back outside. Her neck still stung from where Dominic had practically bitten her, and she still couldn't believe it. Did Romain really think that he'd interrupted them lovemaking?

Forcing herself not to let a wave of self-pity engulf her, Sorcha called on all her professional pride and somehow got through the rest of the day. When they wrapped she stuck close to Val, and made sure she was on a boat with him. Dark shades covered her bruised eyes. Her mouth was a grim line. When she got off the boat and she heard a familiar voice behind her she stopped, but didn't turn around. Her slim shoulders were rigid with tension.

Romain came and stood in front of her. She

could see the rest of the crew walking away towards the hotel.

'You can avoid me all you want, Sorcha, but ultimately you won't be able to. You know that, don't you? And you *will* tell me what was going on with Dominic.'

She said nothing. Didn't move. If she had looked she'd have seen his jaw clench angrily at her stony silence.

Romain could see her throat work. Dark shades covered her eyes, and he nearly moved to take them off but at the last minute didn't. Almost as though he was afraid of what he might see…?

Instead he cupped a hand around her jaw, felt the delicate line and saw a pulse jump in response.

'Be down in the lobby for dinner at seven.' His voice was silky, deadly. 'And if you're not I will come and get you.'

That evening Sorcha stepped out of the lift at seven on the dot. She was dressed traditionally in a *salwaar kameez* with her hair pulled back, plain hoop earrings, and she had her glasses on. Protective armour.

Romain watched her approach and felt the familiar tightening happen in his body at the way the black material clung and curved around her body, the tight trousers under the tunic making her legs look long and slim. *Tonight* he would have her. Make her pay.

To Sorcha's intense relief she saw the rest of the crew and remembered that they were all going for dinner together. A reprieve. She made for Val, seeking protection but Romain blocked her before she could get to him.

He could see the frustration on her face, but he took her arm, and unless she wanted to create a scene Sorcha would have to leave it there. He made a joke with Simon, and then led the way down the street to a beautiful restaurant on the shores of the lake.

When Sorcha saw that Romain meant to have her sit next to him, and that Dominic looked likely to be on the other side of her, it was too much. She didn't care. She reacted on pure, desperate impulse and grabbed Romain's hand, making him look at her with surprise, his dark brows drawing together.

She entreated with her eyes, with all she had. It was the first thing she'd said to him all day and her voice sounded unbearably husky. 'Please. I don't want to sit next to him.'

She couldn't stop a shudder running through her, and Romain's frown drew even deeper as he noticed the minute movement. He looked to his side and saw Dominic taking a seat. For some reason, and not wanting to look too closely at why, he just nodded perfunctorily and let himself sit between Dominic and Sorcha.

An hour later Sorcha was pushing food around her plate. It was still heaped high with food that she couldn't touch, because her insides were churning so much.

'Smile, Sorcha, you look as if you're going to the

gallows. And you haven't eaten all day. You should make some effort.'

She cast a quick glance to Romain on her left. 'Don't tell me you're concerned?'

'Not at all,' he said easily, and draped an arm along the back of her chair, making her pulse trip predictably. 'You're going to need your energy for later…that's all.' And he took a studied sip from his wine glass.

Sorcha gripped the napkin that was on her lap and twisted it.

He got caught in a conversation with Simon across the table, and Sorcha turned with relief to Val, who was on her other side. He was looking at her with a concerned face.

'What's up, Sorch? Every time I look at you you're either flushed like you have a fever or deathly pale…'

She forced a smile. 'Nothing. Just tired, I guess.'

Val jerked his head in the direction of Romain. 'Well, he's been about as subtle as a dog marking his territory.'

Sorcha's spine straightened. 'I don't know what—'

Val snorted. '*Please*. From day one he's marked you as his.' He took her hand under the table and said in a serious voice under his breath, 'Sorch, I mean this in the best possible way, but you are not like the women he goes for. I've seen the casualties of that man dumped by the wayside, and it's not pretty.'

Sorcha felt hysteria not too far from the surface. 'Val—'

'Just…be careful. That's all I'm saying. I don't want to see you get hurt…'

As Val gave her hand a quick squeeze and turned away, Sorcha had to swallow painfully. *Too late for that.* If Romain had his way she'd become his mistress tonight, and be well on the way to becoming his next casualty.

With an abrupt movement she stood up. Romain seized her wrist in a lightning-fast grip. Nobody else seemed to have noticed, but she glared down at him. 'What do you think you're doing, Romain?'

'Where do you think you're going?'

'The toilet—if I may?' She arched a brow.

He glowered up at her, but finally released her and watched her every step of the way as she left.

When she came back he looked at her suspiciously. The reality was so far from what he obviously imagined it was laughable, and she wondered just what she was really doing protecting Lucy. Was the thought of Romain being antagonistic somehow easier to deal with than Romain charming her to seduce her? An uncomfortable prickling assailed her, and she knew she didn't want to look at that.

A splitting headache made her temples throb, and she knew it was from the tension and stress.

Romain looked at her as she pinched the bridge of her nose. He felt irritation rise. Big, wary blue eyes snagged his then, and his breath caught for a second in his throat. God, but she was beautiful.

Sorcha met his grey fathomless gaze head-on. She

had to at least try. 'I'm going to go back to the hotel. I'm tired and I have a headache.'

Romain used every bit of will-power to control the carnal urge to just carry her off then and there. He would not let her reduce him to such base behaviour. He shook his head. 'You're not going anywhere until I say so, and I am not ready to leave.'

Sorcha leant in towards him, agitated. His gaze dropped to the shadowy line of her cleavage under the V of the top. His body hardened in anticipation.

'I'm not a prisoner, you know.'

He looked at her intently. 'No…there's another word for what you are…'

Sorcha sagged back and fell silent.

An hour later Sorcha looked around her in dismay. Somehow someone had persuaded everyone to go to a small bar not far from where they were staying, and even though she dreaded going back to the hotel, and hadn't really contemplated what would happen when she did, she wished she was anywhere but there. With everyone getting drunk around her— apart from Romain, of course, who was in complete control, and disconcertingly as at home here as he had been in five-star surroundings—Sorcha felt absurdly sober.

He was talking to Simon at the bar. The laughing and shouting was grating on her nerves. And a jukebox had started up playing Bollywood songs. Normally she loved them, but right now they sliced through her head. Dominic and Lucy were messing with the playlist, and Sorcha had just about had enough.

She got up and went to leave, not caring any more what Romain might say. Sure enough, just as she was about to walk out, she felt a firm grip on her hand. It set little fires racing up and down her arm.

'Look, Romain, I've had enough. I've got a splitting headache.'

The noise *was* intense with the music playing. Romain was about to say something, but just as he opened his mouth to speak the song on the jukebox finished. And before he could say a word, into the brief silent interlude between that and the next song Dominic's voice sounded across the small bar, clear as a bell and loudly indiscreet.

So drunk or high that he was unaware of the music stopping, he was shouting into Lucy's ear. '…can't believe the stupid bitch took that coke off you and gave you a lecture. Who does she think she is? Holier-than-thou cow. Surprised she didn't go running straight to lover boy to dob you in…'

Dominic kept talking, totally oblivious to the fact that everyone had gone completely quiet and was privy to his conversation.

As if in slow motion, Sorcha watched Romain take in the words, the expressions crossing his face. With a strangled cry she pulled her hand free and ran.

CHAPTER TWELVE

'Sorcha, let me in.'

Sorcha stood in her room, arms around her belly, her breath still harsh. She'd run all the way back to the hotel. When his knock had come on her door, she'd jumped. Maybe if she just—

'Sorcha, I know you're in there. And if you don't open the door I will knock it down.'

She could hear it in his voice. He would. She walked slowly towards the door and inexplicably felt as if shifting sands were beneath her feet. Her mind raced. What did this mean? Did he believe what he'd heard? Her headache pounded with a vengeance.

With a deep, shaky breath, her heart pumping, she slid the bolt back and opened the door. Romain loomed tall and dark and powerful. Sorcha stepped back. She couldn't take her eyes from his, they were staring at her with such intensity.

Romain came in and shut the door behind him, resting his tall frame against it. His face was implacable. He folded his arms across his chest. In dark trousers and a dark shirt he was overpoweringly sexy and dangerous to Sorcha. She backed away, further into the room.

'Why?' was all he said at first.

Sorcha fancied for a moment that she'd missed the first part of his question. When her mouth opened but nothing came out, he stepped away from the door.

He spoke again. 'Why did you do it? Why did you protect her?'

Sorcha's head swam. He *believed* her?

'I… I…' She shook her head. It was too much to take in.

He started pacing back and forth, and the tension in his form radiated out from his body and enveloped her. She felt the bed behind her and sagged onto it, looking at him helplessly.

He stopped in front of her and she had to look up.

'Sorcha. Please tell me why you would protect Lucy. Why didn't you just tell me that *she* was the one with the drugs?'

Something desperate in his voice caught on her insides and twisted them. She shook her head again and gave a tiny shrug.

'I'm sorry…' Her voice came out faintly. 'I just…'

He came down on his haunches before her. Sorcha gulped at the light in his eyes. With just one low lamp on in the room, all the lines in his face were thrown into sharp relief.

'It looked so bad. And I thought…I didn't think you would believe me. Not after…not after everything else. I didn't want her to get into trouble. She's just a kid.' Sorcha shrugged again and said huskily, 'I guess I felt I had nothing to lose.'

He looked at her for a long moment and then stood again, hands on hips. 'I can't believe you let me think that… *Why* would you do it? Why wouldn't you defend yourself?'

Why would you let me believe that about you? The words resounded in Romain's head, compounding the awful clawing guilt he felt. The shock from hearing Dominic's careless words still reverberated through his body. The awful sinking in his belly when he'd confronted the pair as soon as Sorcha had left the bar. He'd known the truth as soon as he'd really focused on them. The scene with her and Dominic earlier flashed into his head, and the other man's behaviour all day…it all took on a new light. He felt sick.

Sorcha stood then too, and paced away from him, agitation marking her jerky movements. She turned and faced him. 'Admit it, Romain, catching me with a gram of coke in my back pocket is something you've imagined could be a possibility from the start—isn't it?'

He looked uncomfortable for a second, and nodded briefly, tersely.

She threw her arms wide and laughed harshly. 'See? I knew how bad it looked, and I *knew* what had happened—never mind how it looked to you! And what if I *had* blamed Lucy yesterday? How would that have appeared on top of everything else? To be blaming someone as young and innocent as her…'

His mouth twisted. Who is anything but…'

Sorcha smiled a little sadly. 'Lucy *is* just young and silly. Dominic has turned her head, and in this business it's all too easy to follow someone's lead.' Sorcha's voice grew hesitant. 'What are you going to do with them?'

Romain ran a hand through his hair and looked very weary all of a sudden. 'They're in no state to be coherent now. I'm going to fire Dominic…' He shrugged. 'And give Lucy the option of staying on or going. As you say, she is young, and thanks to you she didn't actually take anything. Is that OK with you?'

'That's fair, I think,' Sorcha said quietly, a little stunned that he was giving her any say. 'Dominic was the real problem, not her, and maybe this will teach her a lesson.'

He moved closer to her and Sorcha's breath snagged. The energy in the room became heavy with *something*.

'When you asked me that day in Dublin if I'd ever believe you'd never touched drugs…'

Sorcha held her breath.

'You haven't, have you?'

There was a huge black hole opening up under Sorcha. Somewhere she'd avoided visiting for a long time. And for the first time she knew she couldn't avoid it. Very slowly, she shook her head, her eyes never leaving his. She saw some strength in them, something to cling onto. Defied telling herself that it was *him*.

He came closer. 'So what happened in London?'

A bubble seemed to surround them. The outside world didn't exist. Sorcha was looking into grey eyes so intense that she was losing her soul.

'I told you about what happened after my father died…'

Romain nodded, coming closer again, not breaking eye contact. Not letting her be distracted.

And in that moment, all of a mere split second in time, Sorcha made a subconscious decision.

'It wasn't as simple as that.'

'Go on.'

Her hands twisted in front of her. 'After my father died I found my birth certificate in his study at home. I found out that my mother…the person I'd always known as my mother…was in fact *not*.'

There. It was out. And Romain was still looking at her, moving ever closer. Soon he would be able to reach out and touch her. That made Sorcha speak again, as if to keep him back. Space.

'My real mother was in fact my father's secretary. Irish, not Spanish. She had no other family and she died in childbirth with me. When the hospital called looking for her next of kin, who she had listed as my father, my mother found out what had been going on. *She* hadn't been able to have any more children after complications with my brother's birth, so she decided to take me in as her own.'

Her face was so pale it looked like alabaster in the dim light. 'The pain of not being able to have more children far outweighed the pain of her husband's infidelity.'

Romain was so close she could breathe in his smell, and she felt dizzy. Even dizzier when he took her hand and led her over to the couch in the corner to sit down. Sorcha only noticed then how shaky she was.

'And that day in London? When the photographers found you unconscious in the street?'

Sorcha felt numb. The words came out, but she wasn't really aware of saying them and knew that she had gone inwards somewhere.

'That day…was the last straw.' She couldn't look at him. Couldn't launch straight into a bald explanation without going back a little first.

'I'd felt so all over the place, and Katie had done her best to try and comfort me, but…' She looked up then, and Romain had to take in a breath when he saw the pain in her eyes, 'Can you imagine what it was like to discover that you hadn't been who you thought you were? I spent my whole life believing that woman was my mother—that I was half-Spanish…' She gave a strangled half-laugh. 'I mean it's ridiculous. If you saw my brother he looks more Spanish than Irish, and me…' She gestured with a shaking hand to herself.

She took a shuddering breath and went on, too far gone to stop now. 'I shut Katie out. Completely. She was my best friend and I ignored her for weeks. She knew those guys were bad news. And so did I, underneath it all, but I was just…so angry, so confused. I can see now that it was a cry for attention. My crush on Christian was all the kick I needed to be led astray. But, despite my brave show of rebellion, I was terrified of them, really. Of that world, the hedonistic way they behaved.'

'What happened…?'

'We were at a party in another model's house.' Her eyes beseeched him. She wanted him to understand. 'I felt so lost in my desperation to feel part of *something*—anything. I'd managed to convince them I was one of them…but in reality I was hiding drinks, throwing them into plants, pretending to get drunk…If they took drugs I'd act all blasé like I wasn't in the mood. As if they bored me. I hadn't slept with Christian, and was feeling more and more uncomfortable with it all…*him*…and he was getting increasingly pushy.' She took a deep breath. 'At the party, I overheard him tell a friend about how he'd spiked another girl's drink, and then…' she shuddered minutely '…what he'd done to her. I knew right then that I wanted out. It had gone too far. But, as if he *knew*, he came and handed me a drink. He stood there… wouldn't leave until I'd drunk it. By then, I was really terrified. I could feel the effects straight away. I pretended I had to go to the loo and called Katie…'

Sorcha sighed deeply and felt a calmness move through her whole body, as if telling this was somehow exorcising something within her. Romain was still looking at her intently. She seemed to draw strength from it, from him.

'When Katie came I was unconscious in a bedroom…on my own. Somehow she managed to get me outside. She had to leave me for a minute, while she looked out for the ambulance… The paparazzi knew the house as a hangout for models, and they were lying in wait—especially so soon after that other girl—'

'I remember,' he said grimly.

She looked at him warily. 'That's it…That's the sordid and very sad truth. I was naïve, silly—'

Romain put a finger to her mouth. 'No. You were reacting to extreme circumstances. They merely offered you the comfort you thought you needed. But all along, Sorcha, you stayed true to yourself.'

She looked at him and felt like crying. To distract him and herself from the rising tide of emotion, she got up and went into the bathroom.

Romain watched her go, his whole world imploding from the inside out.

She returned and held out the small bottle of pills. He frowned and took them, looking at her warily.

'Homeopathic tablets for prickly heat rash. I take them whenever I go to a hot country because I react to the sun. That's the sum total of my drug use—apart from perhaps paracetamol. I've never even smoked a cigarette.'

He handed her back the bottle and stood stiffly. He'd never felt at such a loss. Had never been in this situation.

His accent was pronounced. 'Sorcha…'

Suddenly she couldn't bear to see him like this. She was just as much to blame. 'Romain, it's fine—'

'It's not fine.' His hand slashed the air. 'If I'd known these things…'

'You didn't know because I didn't tell you—or try to defend myself.'

He looked at her darkly. In a way it had been so much easier yesterday, when he had believed her guilt, to take her in his arms and tell her that he was going to take her as his mistress. But now…things had shifted. Were different. Or were they?

He reached out a hand to tuck some hair behind her ear. He saw how her body tensed, her breathing changed, her eyes widened. Stepping close to her, breathing in her own evocative scent, he could feel it wrapping around his senses, making his body tight with need. His hands lifted and he took off her glasses.

Sorcha's hands came up automatically, but Romain was too quick. The glasses were gone. On the couch beside them. Then his hand was at the back of her head, threading through her hair, unravelling the strands, taking out the elastic band. She put a hand on his to stop him—and that was a mistake. Because she felt the strong bones, the hairs on his skin, felt the pulse thundering. Like her own. Her mouth felt dry.

'What are you doing?' she croaked out.

With a fluid, easy move he pulled her into his body. He stared down into her eyes with an ardour that made it hard to concentrate, that drove everything out of her mind. And she found herself clinging onto it.

She asked again, 'What are you doing?'

His answer was to pull her into him even more, tight against his body, where it felt as if they were joined at every conceivable point.

He bent his head and his breath feathered close to her ear, making her skin tingle all over. 'I told you I'd take you as my mistress…though I meant it as a form of punishment… I still want you, Sorcha…but this time it'll be purely for pleasure.'

And before she could emit a word or a sound he'd taken her mouth with his, and nothing existed but this—the physical reality of Romain de Valois kissing her as if she was the only woman on the planet. Everything was in that kiss. The apology he hadn't articulated, the pent-up passion that had existed since the moment she'd seen him across the room in New York.

Sorcha felt her insides melt and come back to quivering life. The enormity of what she'd just shared was too much…too cerebral. She needed the physical, *welcomed* the physical. Her arms went up and twined around his neck. She imagined that not even a feather would pass between them. And *there*, against the apex of her thighs, she could feel him, hot and heavy and hard.

'Oh…' she breathed, her own body reacting with

spectacular swiftness. She could feel herself grow damp, and colour scorched her cheeks.

He pulled back and brushed a tendril of hair off her cheek. '*Oh*…is right…' he said huskily.

And then, as if answering some plea she wasn't even aware of articulating, he bent his head and his mouth met hers again. There was no hesitation, no thought other than *this*. Now. Here. This man. This insanity where all rational thought flew out of the window.

She groaned deep in her throat when she felt him pull her even tighter, deeper. Cradled in his lap, she moved her hips in a minutely experimental gesture. He pulled back, breathing raggedly.

'Do you know what you're doing?'

She looked up, mute, her lips feeling plump and bruised, tingling. She longed to taste him again.

With one move he'd taken her into his arms and walked over to the bed which was highlighted by the moonlight streaming into the room. He laid her down and she watched as he undid the buttons on his shirt, then his torso was revealed, and even though she'd seen it before she took an intake of breath at the sheer perfection.

'Now you… I need to see you…'

Sorcha felt like a twig in a burning rapid. Something was trying to impinge on her consciousness, but she couldn't let it. Mustn't let it.

Very reverently, Romain came down beside her and started to lift the tunic of the *salwaar kameez*. Sorcha shifted her hips and lifted her arms, and it slipped over her head. Now her torso was bare, apart from her black lacy bra. Her skin looked incredibly white against the material. Romain was staring at her, and she felt her nipples tighten painfully.

He ran a hand over her stomach, to rest it under the curve of one breast. Her breath was growing more and more ragged. Keeping his hand there, he bent his head again, and when their lips met she strained upwards, her tongue finding and meeting his, tangling and tasting in a feverish dance. And when his hand moved up to cup her breast, to run a thumb-pad over one engorged tip, she almost cried out. She had *never* felt this before. And it was here, with this man, where her awakening was taking place.

With those thoughts reality intruded.

Romain's mouth was blazing a trail of hot kisses down her neck, down to where she wanted nothing more than for him to find that tingling point, suck it into his mouth. And she knew if he did that she'd be lost.

Going against every cell in her body, with weak, ineffectual arms, she started to push at Romain's formidable shoulders. For a moment he did nothing, his mouth still making its way ever downwards and Sorcha despaired of getting him to move. She just knew he had to…she wasn't ready for this yet. There was no doubting where this was going to end if she didn't stop it now.

'No… *No!* Romain—stop, please…'

One hand was around her ribs, just under her breast, and his mouth was a breath away from one aching

hard nipple. She could have wept with frustration—
but there was too much at stake and if they went any
further she'd have to explain…the worst bit of all…

CHAPTER THIRTEEN

'WHAT—what is it?' His voice was hoarse, his breathing jagged. She could feel his bare chest rise and fall against her side.

She turned her head, fighting back sudden tears. Then she pushed his hands away and sat up, moving back, taking her top and putting it over her breasts. Her hair fell around her shoulders.

What the hell was going on? Romain couldn't figure the lightning-fast change and went to reach for Sorcha again, his fingers itching with the need to touch, caress. He was on fire.

She scooted back even further, her eyes huge in the dim light. 'No! Don't touch me.'

Such panic laced her voice that Romain jack-knifed off the bed and switched on another lamp, coming to stand with hands on his hips. He looked angry and aroused and very intimidating. Sorcha swallowed miserably.

'I'm sorry...I just can't do this. With you.'

He ran a hand through his hair. 'What are you

talking about Sorcha? If not me then who? I don't see you burning up for anyone else's touch.'

And the thought of her doing this with anyone else made him almost incandescent with rage.

She closed her eyes for a second to block out his potent image. Of course she didn't *burn up* for anyone else. There never had been anyone else, and at this moment in time she couldn't ever imagine feeling this way about anyone else. But he couldn't know how deeply he'd drawn her into his web of seduction.

'I just can't...'

Romain was pacing up and down. His shirt was flapping around his chest and Sorcha wished he'd stop and do it up—anything so that she wouldn't have to look at him and get heated up all over again. He went and leant against the patio door, arms crossed, muscles bunching in a way that made him even more provocative. Sorcha avoided his gaze, holding her top in front of her like a lifeline.

He stepped out of the shadow and he saw how Sorcha shrank back into the bed ever so slightly. He also saw the flare in her eyes, and the way they ran hungrily down his chest. Her hands were shaking. But, as he came closer he saw the shadows in those clear blue depths. That vulnerability hit him square between the eyes—*again*.

'Why, Sorcha? Just tell me why?'

Sorcha looked at him then, and fire lit her eyes. She felt so transparent at this moment, and she hated that this man had done it to her. Somewhere along

the way he'd morphed from arch nemesis into…
something else, and the thought of what that might
be made her very scared.

'Why do you have to know everything about me?'
she asked jaggedly, conveniently forgetting her own
eager response just moments before. 'Can't you just
let me be?'

He came down on the bed beside her, and held her
with one arm when she would have scooted away. It
was warm and heavy against her skin. She could
already feel how her body was responding—the
tightness in her belly, her lips tingling in anticipation
of his touching hers again—and she didn't just want
him to kiss her mouth. She wanted him to kiss
her…*everywhere*.

She closed her eyes weakly. Tonight seemed to be
the night when some god had determined that she
would be torn down and built up again, and she knew
that somehow some very cowardly part of her had
clung to his bad opinion of her, had taken Lucy's guilt
on as her own in order to avoid this… Because if he
suspected the worst, then he'd never see the real her.

She opened her eyes. His face was too close, but
she knew he wouldn't be moving anywhere.

'Dites moi pourquoi…?'

Tell me why…?

Sorcha turned her head away. She felt as bared as
she'd ever been, because what she was about to tell
him *no one* knew. Words came out in a rush. Her
voice was none too steady

'Because…I haven't done this before…and I don't even know…if I'm a virgin.'

She felt tears spring into her eyes and shut them tight. Her jaw wobbled. She'd heard his swift intake of breath and then nothing. Maybe he'd go? Leave? Maybe taking a virgin was a step too far for someone like—?

A warm hand came to her jaw and pulled it round gently. She kept her eyes squeezed shut.

'Sorcha. Open your eyes.' His voice was husky.

She opened her eyes and knew they must be swimming as he was a blur in her vision.

He was looking at her with that intense ardour again, and it confused her.

'Do you want to tell me why you think you might not be a virgin?'

She shook her head.

He came up closer, dwarfing her body with his own, and her eyes followed him helplessly.

'I think it's time you told someone. It might as well be me.'

His words were so matter-of-fact that they actually distracted her. Sorcha looked at him, as if searching for some hidden meaning, and finally she realised that he was right. Sooner or later she would be in this situation again and right now her body was burning up for a fulfilment that only he could provide.

She took a deep breath before she spoke her next words. 'When I came to in the hospital when the drug had worn off, I knew that I'd blacked out for a bit before Katie got to me. I tried to stay awake for as long as I could.' She shrugged. 'I never said anything…but just…always had a fear that Christian, or someone, might have done something to me and I didn't know…'

He looked at her for a long moment. She couldn't read his expression, but at least it didn't have the horror in it that she'd always imagined she'd be faced with. But then he moved back, and Sorcha felt so bereft it was like a pain cramping her belly.

He got off the bed, his face all shadows and harsh angles in the light. Powerful arms folded across his chest. Driven away again.

Sorcha's body still throbbed and pulsed. But she had to concede the thought of her being a virgin was obviously too much. *She* couldn't even take in all of what she'd just told him, or how wantonly she'd acted… Her whole brain seized up in embarrassment at the thought. Awkwardly she slipped her top back on and stood up from the bed too.

'I'm sorry,' she said stiffly. 'I should have told you before we let things…'

Romain stepped out of the shadows that had concealed him. He'd needed some kind of protection to hide the extent of the pain he knew must be etched on his face at having to stop, his arousal not having abated one bit. And to hide the shock…the need he'd had to comfort her. To think that she was a *virgin* made his blood fizz and jump. The urge he'd had to press her back down and subdue her fears with kisses had been almost overwhelming. But how could he do such a thing after everything she had just told him?

For the first time ever he was putting a woman's emotional needs first, and it made him reel.

He strolled towards her doing up his shirt. She looked so vulnerable and so damned beautiful that his fingers shook on the buttons. He stopped in front of her and willed the heat in his body to cool. He tipped her face up to his and had to stifle a groan. 'Sorcha. I think you've been through a lot.' His mouth twisted. 'Much of it at my hands. Why don't you get some rest?'

That was about all he could manage—because if he didn't leave right now, then he'd tip her back and take her, ready or not. With that in mind, and staying well away from any erogenous zone, he pressed a swift kiss to her forehead.

Sorcha watched him walk away. Bereft didn't even come into it. She felt as if he were tearing out her heart and carrying it with him. Again she had that feeling of needing the physical to counteract the mental...If he walked out through that door, the bubble would burst—whatever *thing* it was that had just happened to make her tell all. To trust him.

He was at the door, and Sorcha felt something fierce and elemental run through her. Needing what she knew only he could offer her, emboldened by everything she'd just shared, she called his name softly. So softly that he didn't stop. His hand was on the knob. But then, as if her call had wound its way through the air between them and reached out to him, he halted for a second.

'Romain…' she said, more strongly this time.

He turned and looked at her. She saw the lines on his face, as if he was making a supreme effort, and she prayed it was what she thought. She'd already revealed so much she felt a little invincible. Bold.

'Don't you *want* to make love to me?'

He turned around and rested his whole body back against the door. He made some kind of inarticulate sound. And then he said, very hoarsely, 'More than you can imagine.'

'Then don't leave.'

'Sorcha…' he said helplessly.

She gripped the bedpost. 'Please, Romain. Don't leave. I need you to…make love to me. I need *you*.' Aghast at her nerve, she said, 'If I could move I'd come over there, but I'm afraid if I do I'll fall down…'

Her heart-aching honesty reached out and grabbed him by the scruff of the neck. As if he'd even stood a chance when he'd heard that soft *Romain*… A heated urgency moved him, a deep throbbing in his veins, and he pushed off the door and within seconds was *there*—Sorcha in his arms, mouths fused, her hands wrapped tight around his waist. He could feel her whole body tremble against his.

He pulled back and looked down for just a moment. He tried to will some sanity into the situation. 'Sorcha…are you sure?'

She just nodded, then reached a hand up and around

the back of his head, pulling him back down to her. 'I've never been more sure of anything in my life.'

That was it. He was gone. Had just been given licence to sate the burning ache in his loins. Before he could even think about it Sorcha had reached down and pulled off her top, dropping it to the floor.

Romain undid the buttons on his shirt, his eyes never leaving hers. With his shirt gone, he pushed her gently back onto the bed. His hand moved down her shoulder, taking her bra strap with it, his other hand taking the other one. He reached under and behind, undid the clasp, and then the wisp of material was gone.

He hovered over her like a Greek god and said, 'Sorcha…just trust me. I won't hurt you.'

She nodded jerkily and fought back tears. His words made a faint alarm go off somewhere, but it was drowned out in the heady clamour of her pulse. This was so far removed from what she had envisaged this moment to be like. Nowhere to be seen was the vaguely insipid man she'd always imagined; gentle, unassuming, sensitive. Instead it was *this* man, who had all those qualities but packaged so much more dynamically. He was larger than life and he had turned her life upside down and inside out. In the space of what must in reality have been just an hour, she'd bared her soul—and now she was about to bare her body completely.

The moment was so huge that she felt faint. To drive it away she reached up and pulled his head down to hers, her mouth searching blindly and finding his, their tongues meeting and meshing. And soon the only thing she could think about was the need that was building inside her that had to be assuaged—*now*.

She felt him undo the tie of her trousers and slip them down her legs. She kicked them off. Then he dealt with his own trousers. And briefs. As he came back down alongside her she caught a glimpse of the visible evidence of his arousal and her insides contracted.

Somehow her pants were gone. She couldn't even remember if she had slipped them off or if Romain had. Their mouths clung. His hand smoothed its way down over her heated flesh, over the swell of her breast, fingers teasing the turgid tip. She rocked against him, seeking and finding that hardness. Hesitantly, she drifted a hand down between them, revelling in the feel of his smooth, silky skin. It felt hot to the touch.

She reached round and felt his behind, one taut, perfect globe, and then one muscled strong thigh. When she felt a hand exploring her belly, going lower, her breath and her wandering hand stopped. With infinite gentleness Romain's fingers threaded through the hair that hid her sex and delved into that place which was moist with her desire.

Her head fell back and he watched her face as his fingers sought and found the secrets of her body. Unconsciously she moved against his hand, seeking more. His thumb rubbed against her clitoris, fingers thrusting in and out. Her hand gripped his thigh and brokenly she begged him. 'Please… Romain…'

So he did. He brought her over the edge. Felt the uncontrollable spasms of her body around his fingers. She trapped his hand with her legs, her body suddenly acutely sensitive and looked up, her cheeks flushed.

Romain smiled and took her hand, brought it down to touch him. Her eyes widened as, with his hand over hers, he let her encircle the hard shaft. 'See what you do to me?'

Heat. All Sorcha could think of was heat and molten blood running through her veins. The desire was building again, spiralling, tightening every part of her. Romain came over her, one thigh between her legs, opening her up to him. Her hand fell away from him as he moved over her fully and the potent heat of him lay between her legs. Where her universe seemed to end and begin.

He pressed a kiss to her lips, a lingering one, and as he did, with his chest against hers, he slid into her tight opening. Sorcha gasped against his mouth. But he didn't break the kiss, and slid a little deeper. Although there was no physical barrier to impede his entry, it was clear that no one had penetrated her like this before now. A fierce, elemental wave of pride and ownership washed through Romain. He finally took his mouth from hers and looked down. He wanted to see her face when he took her, when he was so embedded within her that she wouldn't be able to think of anything else, *anyone* else.

He felt her hands on his back, her legs come up, and with that movement he couldn't help himself sinking deeper. A brief spasm crossed her face and Romain halted immediately, his heart hammering. 'Are you OK?'

She nodded and smiled. 'More than OK… You feel… amazing.'

And then he surged forward again and was there. At the core. At the centre of everything. Sheathed completely in a hot velvet glove of tightness. Holding back from pulling out and driving in again as hard as his body demanded, he controlled his movements. There would be time for that later. When he took her again. At the thought of that, unbelievably his body hardened even more. It made his head spin.

With steady thrusts he pierced Sorcha's flesh again and again. Until she thrashed beneath him. Until her hands pulled at his arms, his shoulders. Until her head was flung back and her chest thrust up and he felt the ripples along his length that told him of her fast-approaching release.

And, because it had taken more strength than he possessed, for those few final moments he gave in to the elemental waves building in his own body. When she cried out her release his own body contracted and then spilled its life seed into her. He slumped over her, breathing harshly.

When Sorcha woke, some hours later, the light of the rising dawn was stealing into the room. She couldn't move. She'd never felt so heavy. Never felt so at peace. Never had a naked man wrapped around her back before, with one big hand cupping her breast.... She felt an inordinate feeling of well-being rush through her. She moved her bottom a little and heard a sleep-rough growl in her ear.

'Stop that. You're going to be sore today…and if you keep doing that I won't be able to stop myself.'

Her cheeks flooded with warmth. Already she could feel his erection pressing insistently against her.

So she turned and faced him. Sleepy grey eyes regarded her with heavy-lidded sensuality. Emotion welled through her like a tidal wave, and she had to stop her hand from reaching out and tracing every line of his exquisite face. It looked even darker, shadowed with a little stubble.

How had they got here? Sorcha coloured again. Well, she knew how they had got *here*, but she had a flash of memory back to New York, remembering the intense attraction and also the intense antipathy. His extreme arrogance. Another wave of tenderness made her feel dizzy for a second, and in that moment she knew it was a much bigger emotion.

It was *love*.

She loved him. He had been witness to her ultimate capitulation. And her redemption. He had made her whole again—given her back her sanity. She now knew that eight years ago *nothing* had happened without her knowledge, and that made her feel giddy with love for this man. It also made her reach out, despite her best intentions, and curl a hand around his neck, bringing his face close to hers.

'Sorcha, what are—?'

She pressed a sweet kiss to his mouth.

And then, so suddenly that it felt almost violent, he pulled back, those grey eyes coldly expressionless. And in a split second he was out of the bed and walking towards the bathroom.

Sorcha lay frozen. The chill in his eyes just now had made a direct hit into her very bones. Snatches and snippets of the previous night sank heavily into her consciousness. She heard the hiss of the shower. Could imagine that tall, lean, finely honed body standing underneath the spray, water sluicing down…

What was she doing? Daydreaming, mooning… Did she want to be lying here like some kind of love-struck groupie when he got out? There had been no tender words this morning—nothing to indicate that this was anything but normal practice for him. The morning after for him was something he was used to. He'd merely done what he'd set out to do—taken her to bed. Hadn't he asserted his intention to do that *no matter what*?

Lying there, stricken, she had to recall with abject horror how she'd told him…*everything*. Absolutely *everything*. There wasn't a part of her, mentally or physically, that this man didn't know. She recalled her rush of love just moments ago and cringed. She'd projected so much more onto their union than he had.

She heard the shower stop. And, with a reflex action so swift she surprised herself, she leapt out of bed, put on her clothes, and was about to leave the room when, with her hand on the door, she realised she was in her own room.

'Going somewhere?' a mocking voice drawled from behind her.

CHAPTER FOURTEEN

SORCHA turned around, her cheeks burning. She felt stiff—literally and emotionally. Nakedly vulnerable.

'I'd like you to leave, please. I have plans for the day, and I have to pack and get ready for Spain.'

She avoided looking at him as he was dressed in nothing but a tiny towel. Baring everything except... Her cheeks burned again as he quite calmly dropped the towel and started to pull on his clothes. He didn't seem to be fazed by her coolness. And that only confirmed her worst fears, suspicions.

He dressed and strolled towards her. But when she would have turned the knob and opened the door he stopped her hand with his. Snaking his other hand around the back of her head, he tilted her head and dropped his mouth onto hers, stealing a kiss that was hot and made her yearn to lean into him, her body already remembering, wanting, aching all over again. But then...he let her go. She opened dazed eyes. His were cool, alert. It almost seemed as if last night had never happened—as if she'd dreamt up Dominic's timely confession, as if the physical had been the only thing.

'As it happens, I have to go on to Madrid ahead of the crew for meetings. I have my private jet waiting at a nearby airfield. Come with me.'

At that moment, as if she'd even needed it, Val's words came back to her like an insidious poison. She was another casualty. Maybe not right at this moment, but any day now.

She shook her head vehemently. 'No. I've booked a day trip. I'll travel with the crew tomorrow.'

He regarded her, and she focused on a point just over his shoulder. She was immovable, tense, waiting for his insistence—which she was sure was coming.

Romain still regarded her. He knew he could persuade her but at that moment something flashed into his head and he went cold.

Sorcha sensed it and looked up, her eyes wary. Guarded.

'We didn't use protection last night.'

Sorcha saw the horrified expression on his face. Felt guilty even though she'd been the innocent one. She couldn't believe she'd let him take such a liberty without even noticing herself. But then, she hadn't been aware of much…

She feigned all the insouciance she could muster. 'Well, I'm assuming that you're clean. And I'm due my period…' She faltered because it inexplicably hurt to admit it. 'Today, actually…' She fought down the bizarre emotion that ripped through her and tossed her head. 'So you don't have to worry…'

Romain was implacable. He just bit out a curt, slightly haughty, 'Of course I'm clean. And that's good…about your period…'

With the atmosphere humming tensely, he opened the door and left. No kiss. Nothing.

Sorcha sagged back when he'd left. His eagerness to leave had left her slightly stunned. The man had her upside down and inside out. And how *could* she have been so remiss as to forget about one of the most basic fundamentals—protection?

Romain looked out of the tiny window by his seat in the luxurious Learjet. In his hand he cradled a glass of neat whisky. The ground dropped away beneath him and he felt numbed, removed from everything. One thing concerned him. One thing consumed him—his body and his mind.

Sorcha Murphy.

He still couldn't believe how wrong he'd got it. *And how right*. He still hadn't really allowed the enormity of what she'd shared with him last night to sink in. The enormity of how he'd contributed to her awful pain eight years ago. How philosophical she'd been, how little anger she'd held…when she had every right to rant and rail. It shook him to his core. And then to find she'd been a virgin…and that he was her first—

His hand clenched around the glass even tighter, knuckles white. He fought to control the intense desire that made his body react like an over-eager teenager. What little control he might have possessed around her before had long gone.

When she had pressed that kiss to his mouth this morning two things had driven him from the bed so fast his head had spun. The first was that he'd never woken wrapped around a woman, *aching* to have her again and again. And the second was that he'd seen something in her eyes that had made him feel something he hadn't felt in a long, long time. Something he'd recognised. Because once he had been the one who had bared his soul, shared his secrets, shared his dreams with someone—and they had not trod softly on them…in fact they had ground them out and used them against him.

But he pictured her face as she had stood by the door…when she'd given him her assurance that she wasn't likely to become pregnant. Sorcha Murphy had looked anything but delicate, fragile, vulnerable. With any other woman he had clarity, he was removed, objective, never so lost in the passion that he became careless.

His hand clenched tighter on the glass. He stopped the churning in his mind but couldn't control his body, which ached to possess her again. His head throbbed.

Sorcha was bone-weary. Everyone was feeling it— along with the long transatlantic journey they'd just made the day before. Today, in Madrid's main square, a huge crowd had turned up to watch them filming.

It was a sequence in which she and Zane joined in with old people waltzing in the square. They were doing it for the last time, and again Sorcha couldn't help her eyes searching...seeking...looking for one person. She felt empty inside. She'd known he was due to be at meetings but still, she had expected— didn't want to say *hoped*—he'd turn up. Was he already off with another woman? She had it bad, and Val's warning kept sounding in her head like a claxon.

'OK, guys—that's a wrap in Madrid. Well done. Travel day tomorrow to Paris. We're leaving at midday sharp.'

Sorcha breathed a sigh of relief and smiled tiredly at Zane. The atmosphere on set had been a million times better since Dominic had disappeared, and a new photographer had arrived to meet them here in Spain. Lucy had obviously had her dressing down from Romain and decided to stay. She'd apologised to Sorcha the previous day, coming to her room not long after Romain had left.

The cars took them back to their sumptuous hotel on a quiet street nearby, and Sorcha took a long, relaxing bath. At least she had something to look forward to for the evening. She pushed all thoughts of Romain out of her head.

An hour later, dressed in a knee-length silk flowery dress and a cardigan, with flat shoes, her hair still damp, and dark glasses, Sorcha emerged from the hotel armed with her guidebook and a map. As she turned to her left and began to walk she didn't see the sleek car pull up, or Romain uncoil from the back seat, see *her* and, with his brows pulling into a frown, dismiss the car and start to follow her.

The tiredness he'd been feeling in every bone had vanished as soon as Romain saw Sorcha emerge from the hotel before him. But she hadn't seen him. She was engrossed in a map and guidebook. It made him feel pettishly impotent. He was used to women looking out for him, waiting for him…*welcoming him*. So he'd decided to follow her—and he didn't look at how this behaviour was such an anomaly to his normal *modus operandi*. It had been too long since India, and the way her hips swayed in the silk dress was making his body react with an annoying degree of uncontrollable arousal.

He caught another man do a double take as she passed him, and he had to fight the urge to go and claim her, take her hand…

As he struggled to regain control he had to reason with himself. He'd been with women who were more beautiful. Women who were sleek, sophisticated, *experienced*. but there was something—*many things*—about Sorcha that he couldn't figure out. Was that it? Maybe she was just playing him as he'd never been played before? Maybe he was the one who was looking like the complete fool, despite her comparative innocence?

That thought made him stop in his tracks for a second, and he realised he was following a woman like some mad, deranged stalker. When she disappeared from view he fought an intense battle…and let her go.

That night, however, Romain found himself sitting in the dim light of the hotel foyer. He'd knocked on Sorcha's door. She hadn't been there. She was obviously still out. Feeling more and more agitated, kicking himself for not following her earlier, Romain now nursed a stiff whisky and waited.

And then, with that husky laugh preceding her, he saw her walk in through the open doors. But she wasn't alone. She was with a man. A tall, dark, very handsome man. Recognition hovered on the periphery of Romain's stunned brain, but Sorcha looked up into the man's face and laughed again, looking so *happy*, and then *he* looked down at her as if—

Romain had jerked his body out of the seat so fast his head swam, and the movement brought Sorcha's eyes to his. They widened. Her mouth opened. Her cheeks flushed.

He closed the space between them so fast that Sorcha felt dizzy.

'Romain…' Her heart leapt with a joy she tried to crush. She took in his features as avidly as if they'd been separated for weeks, not just a couple of days.

The man beside her took her arm out of his and Sorcha's focus came back. She saw how Romain transferred his gaze to glare at him. They matched each other height for height, build for build.

A dryly amused, deep voice spoke from beside her. 'Sorch, do you want to introduce me to this gentleman who looks as if he wants to kill me?'

Somehow she found her voice.

'Romain de Valois, please meet Tiarnan Quinn… my brother.'

The rush of relief that ripped through Romain nearly floored him. Tiarnan must have seen something, because he deftly manoeuvred the three of them over to a couch and ordered a round of drinks.

Moments later Romain still felt a little shaky, and sipped at his drink with studied carefulness. Of course he knew Tiarnan Quinn. Who didn't? The man was a multibillionaire—an entrepreneur who had made a name for himself as someone who tore down countless companies only to build them back up again. Sorcha's words came back to him. That was why they looked so different. Her brother had inherited his mother's Spanish genes. But she'd never mentioned just *who* he was.

That caught Romain up short too. In his experience if people knew other people with power, not to mention were *related* to them, they invariably used it shamelessly—and Tiarnan Quinn was one of the most recognised, powerful people in the world.

Tiarnan stuck out a hand, making a proper introduction, and the tension dissipated, Sorcha watched as the two very Alpha males bonded in true male fashion. Recognising each other's pedigree. As only men in their rarefied circles would. It would have amused her if she hadn't still been getting over the shock of how she'd reacted to seeing Romain.

After a conversation she couldn't even remember, everything still a blur, Tiarnan got up to leave. Sorcha held onto him in a tight hug, as though loath to let him go. He looked down at her with concern in his eyes, and she forced herself to smile as if nothing was wrong. He'd already spent too much time worrying about her, feeling guilty for not having been there for her all those years ago. And he had a difficult nine-year-old daughter. She didn't want to add to his burdens.

When he'd gone, Sorcha ignored Roman and walked resolutely to the elevator. He was right behind her. When the door closed, the space seemed unbearably intimate. She determined not to give any indication of her bone-deep response to seeing him.

Think of his attitude that morning. Think of his attitude, his coolness—

Romain hit the stop button and the lift juddered to a halt. Sorcha's eyes flew to his.

'What do you think—?'

He reached for her, and against her volition she found herself in his arms. He bent his head to hers and took her mouth with such sure mastery that she didn't have a hope of pretending this wasn't what she wanted too.

Things escalated with scary swiftness. There was no hesitation. The temperature in the small enclosed space soared. Sorcha's hands dragged off his jacket, searched for and opened buttons on his shirt, pulled it out of his trousers. She needed to feel flesh, and when she did her hands ran round his back, her legs weakened.

Romain's own hands ran urgently wherever they could. The silk material of the dress slipped and slid through his fingers, thwarting his efforts. With a guttural moan he lifted his mouth from hers and with very little finesse tackled the offending buttons, just managing to hold back from ripping them open. Eventually he could see a pale swell, and like a man starved of water he pulled down the lace of her bra. Her breast sprang free and he bent his head, taking the puckered tight peak into his mouth.

Sorcha's hand was on his head, his fingers clasped tight around his skull. She sagged back against the wall of the elevator with her eyes half open. And what she saw in the mirror opposite served as a harsh wake-up call.

Romain's dark head at her breast, her eyes feverish with brightness, a flush extending from her chest and up, her dress half off, his own shirt flapping open, his jacket on the ground. She felt his hand snake down and reach under her dress, moving up her leg, and with an abrupt move she pushed him back and stood away, breathing heavily. Everything in disarray.

'Stop… We can't…'

Fiercely aroused grey eyes glittered down at her. Her mouth felt swollen and plump. She could feel the wet aching heat between her legs—knew she was so ready that all he'd have to do would be to strip off her panties, lift her up against the wall—

'And why would that be, when it seems to be an inevitability between the two of us if we're alone for more than a second?' His voice sounded harsh, taut with need. And it echoed through her, making a lie of her words.

Weakly she shut her eyes and started to do up her dress. Thanked God for divine intervention. 'We can't because I have my period...I *told* you.'

And you were relieved—don't you remember?

Sorcha looked at him almost accusingly.

Romain ran a hand through his hair and had to feel relief that some kind of sanity had broken through, because he knew that if she hadn't stopped them right now they *would* be making love in a lift. And he had to realise too that, yet again, he was without protection. And that it most likely wouldn't have stopped him this time either...

'Yes. You're right.' With a calm he didn't feel, he started to do up his own clothes. And then, when they were ready, standing almost like two strangers, he pressed the button for her floor and the lift ascended again. The moment of insanity gone.

Romain remonstrated with himself. He couldn't go on like this. It was too...out of control. Seconds in a lift and he'd been pawing at her like some lust-crazed schoolboy!

He was back in time to a place he thought he'd

shut out for good. *Again.* In the presence of *this* woman.

That time—the only other time he'd felt the same sensation of being out of control—he'd got it back by shutting off his heart. He liked his life just the way it was. He could cope with a certain level of dissatisfaction. Because the alternative if he pursued this— pursued *her*—He shut down that line of thinking.

Sorcha Murphy could *not* be the only woman he would desire ever again…and he would prove it.

When the bell pinged softly, Sorcha flinched. She got out without even looking at Romain. Her insides churning, her belly tight. And he said nothing. The door slid shut again behind her.

Back in her own room, Sorcha stripped and crawled into bed. She felt cold. The intense white heat that had consumed them from nowhere in the lift had gone and left her aching with unfulfilled desire. She had stupidly imagined, *hoped*, that the rush of love she had felt in India after sleeping with Romain had been just an extreme response to having shared so much of herself. To baring herself so completely.

But seeing him tonight—the way she'd reacted then…the way she'd gone up in flames in the lift— all that told her that her response had been all too real. She buried her head in her pillow to stop the weak, silent tears. She hadn't learnt a thing. The first person to come along and make her open up and she'd fallen for them like a devoted puppy.

Silly and naïve all over again.

To go and fall in love with Romain de Valois, of all people. The one man in the world who would not, *could* not, love her back.

CHAPTER FIFTEEN

'OK, Sorcha, now look at him as if you really love him.'

Sorcha was doing her best. In a street full of extras, in the middle of Paris, she was looking into Zane's eyes. But instead of blue all she could see was grey. And all she could feel was those grey eyes boring into her from the other side of the street.

'OK, and now, Zane, take her in your arms and kiss her.'

Zane pulled her into his arms, his consummate professionalism making it smooth and graceful, but Sorcha felt as stiff as a board. And when Zane pressed his lips to hers she was glad that the camera was favouring him, because she could feel a wave of revulsion come over her.

Romain watched from behind the monitor. A red mist had descended on his vision as he had watched Sorcha laughing and joking with Zane. And now she was kissing him. Did she have to look so good in his arms? Did he have to grab her so close? The thought of Zane feeling her curves pressed up against him had Romain ready to call out, the job forgotten, the reason they were even there forgotten. But just then Simon did it for him and told them to cut. Romain trembled slightly. Still out of control for this woman, despite his best efforts.

They'd been in Paris for almost four days. They were running behind schedule because of a problem with some of the clothes not being available, and then a problem with the specialised camera that Simon was using. But this was it—the last shot.

When they finally agreed they were happy with everything, they called a wrap and released all the extras. Everyone started packing up, and Sorcha disappeared to her dressing room in a nearby hotel with Zane and the stylist.

She and Zane had done a sequence of shots earlier, with a one-year-old baby girl and a five-year-old boy. It had affected Sorcha far more deeply than she would have thought, bringing up a hitherto non-existent biological clock, and she'd found herself very studiously avoiding Romain's laser-like gaze. Kate was the one who'd always wanted a family, not her. What was wrong with her?

'Are you staying around for the party tomorrow night, Sorch?'

She looked at Val, arching her brow. Her whole body ached with tiredness. And ached with the knowledge that Romain had obviously decided he'd had enough of their…whatever it was. He hadn't made contact once since arriving in Paris. She was already a casualty.

'They're throwing a wrap party to say thanks, and they're inviting some bigwigs to see a very rough cut of what we've shot.'

Sorcha shook her head. She couldn't imagine anything worse than hanging around for longer than absolutely necessary. And she had to get home for the opening of the outreach centre in two weeks' time.

'No…I'm going to try and get a flight home in the morning.'

'So things didn't—?'

She halted Val's words with a quick, curt, 'No.'

The last thing she wanted too was to see an I-told-you-so look on anyone's face.

When Sorcha got back to the hotel a little later she was so tired all she wanted to do was order Room Service and crawl into bed. She had a shower and felt a little better, putting on a soft voluminous robe and wrapping her hair in a towel. When the knock came, she went and answered, assuming it to be the food she had ordered.

The breath whooshed from her body when she saw Romain on the other side, one arm leaning on the doorjamb, the other stuck in his jeans pocket.

She went to slam the door on a reflex, but Romain stuck his foot in the way.

'Excuse me,' she said as coldly as she could, her insides a mass of quivering nerve-ends. 'I'm expecting Room Service and then I'm going to bed. So if you wouldn't mind moving your foot…'

'Of course.' He obliged happily, but instead of moving it and stepping away from the door, he moved it and stepped inside.

Sorcha gaped at his audacity and crossed her arms over her chest, glad of the huge robe which concealed how her body was responding.

'I meant for you to leave.'

He leant against the back of the door and his eyes raked her up and down. 'I've missed you, Sorcha…'

Sorcha snorted, and words trembled on her lips, her mind swirling with confusion. Even though she was doing her best to act cool and insouciant, to push him away, she was hurting badly—and that largely had to do with something someone had left out for her tin the dressing room. It rose up and she spoke without thinking.

'Could've fooled me. We've been in Paris for four days now. If you've missed me so much, maybe you should have taken *me* out to dinner last night instead of Solange Colbert.'

Romain tensed. 'How did you hear about that?'

Sorcha cursed her runaway mouth. Would she never learn? And she cursed whoever it was again for leaving that paper just where she'd see it, with all the subtlety of a brick. And then she felt too angry to care.

'Romain, please don't insult my intelligence; she's one of France's most famous models. It's all over the French press today. Very cosy pictures.'

'My relationship with her is none of your business.'

'Well, evidently,' Sorcha spat out.

He advanced towards her with silky deadliness. Sorcha backed away. 'Don't come near me.'

'Why?' he taunted. 'Because you can't trust yourself?'

'Don't be ridiculous. I trust myself fine. I'm just not interested in another woman's cast-offs.'

'And if I told you nothing happened?'

'I wouldn't believe you.'

He shrugged, still advancing, 'Well, then, I'm afraid you're just going to have to believe what you want.'

Sorcha's knees hit the back of the bed and she staggered slightly.

'Get away from me.' But her voice was breathier this time. He filled her vision, her senses, her mind— and, God help her, she wanted him to fill her body.

'I haven't seen you since we got to Paris because I've been caught up in unavoidable work meetings... and in wrapping up this job.'

A voice mocked him. *Liar...you tried to stay away and it didn't work...*

Sorcha tilted her small chin defiantly. 'You don't have to explain yourself to me. I don't care.'

He continued as if she hadn't spoken. 'Then Solange called me yesterday and asked me out. *Asked me out*. And I went. Do you know why?'

Sorcha shrugged. She couldn't take her eyes off his. He was so close now that she could touch him if she wanted to, and her hands itched.

He sounded almost angry, and the intensity of his

tone was doing something intense to Sorcha's insides.

'Because *you* are everywhere I look. You're in my head, my blood, and it's like a fever. I've never felt this way about anyone and I don't like it.'

'Well, I'm…sorry.'

And then something elemental moved through Sorcha, and she stepped forward so her nose was within centimetres of Romain's chest.

She poked him with a finger and he swayed back slightly. 'Actually, do you know what? I'm *not* sorry. And do you know why? Because I never asked for this. From the word go I told you I didn't want to do this job, but you insisted because you always get your own way. I never asked to be attracted to you. I never asked for you to take me to bed. I never asked to spill my guts. Well, I've had enough, Mr High and Mighty— Mr Confused who doesn't know what he wants—'

'What did you say?' he asked incredulously.

Sorcha was past caring—past being really aware of what she was saying. Her blood was on fire and she was afraid that if she didn't keep talking she'd jump on Romain and beg him to take her right there and then, standing up against a wall.

He stopped backing away and Sorcha looked up, at a loss for words for a second. The air sizzled around them. And then, with a sudden swift movement, Romain had pulled open and yanked down the top of her robe, so she was bared to him from the waist up. Sorcha gasped in shock and outrage, but just as swiftly Romain grabbed her close, taking both of her hands with one of his and anchoring them behind her back.

She struggled fruitlessly, about as effective as a fly on its back, and any more gasps or words of outrage were silenced as his mouth came down on hers and a violent explosion of need erupted in her belly and between her legs.

He lifted his head for a brief moment and said, 'You're wrong. I know exactly what I want, and it's right here in my arms. *Et maintenant, je n'en peux plus…*'

Sorcha opened her mouth to speak, but he stopped any words with his own mouth again. She had a moment of wanting to struggle, but then she became aware of how her breasts were crushed against his chest, the friction of his shirt making her nipples taut and tight with need. The towel had slid off her head and her hair was wet against her back, where his hand was threading through it to the back of her head, urging her closer, angling it for his benefit. Any thought of struggle fled. Instead she wanted to feel him, flesh to flesh. She struggled to get her hands free but he was so strong, so ruthless. His other hand moved down her back, skimming under the robe, loosening it even further until it hung treacherously on her hips. And then with a brief flick of his fingers it fell to the floor completely, and she was naked in his arms, captive to his onslaught.

His hand urged her against him, and she could

feel the heated evidence of his desire through the fabric of his jeans. The friction against her own deeply sensitised body was making her tremble. And then his hand moved up over her waist and higher, around the front, over her belly to the swell of one breast. He still hadn't released her mouth, his tongue and teeth nipping, tracing her full lower lip. Sorcha was dizzy with needs that clamoured through her blood and body like waves pounding against a shore.

When his hand closed around that breast, and his mouth finally left hers to make a sensual passage ever downwards, her legs couldn't hold her up any more. She would have sunk to the floor if not for Romain's arm supporting her. His mouth closed over the tight, turgid peak with an almost savage intensity, and Sorcha couldn't stop herself from crying out. She ached with the need to touch and caress. Her hands being imprisoned was too much of a torture.

'Please…Romain…please…' she begged brokenly, hating the weakness in her voice.

'Please, what?'

'Please…let me go…'

'Never.'

His eyes glittered with glowing silver flames. He did finally release her hands, but only briefly, to carry her over to the bed. He laid her down, stripping off his clothes with indecent haste, and she didn't have time to formulate a word or a thought. He stood before her, a tall, lean bronzed specimen of thrusting male potency. He reached for something in his jeans pocket. *Protection*. He smoothed it on. Even that reminder couldn't cool her blood. Watching him stroke it on made her even hotter.

All she could think was for this moment he was *hers*. She opened her arms to him and he fell on her. They kissed and touched and stroked and smoothed and writhed. Their bodies were slick with sweat. Breath intermingling, short and rapid.

And then he was there, thrusting more deeply than he had done before. Sorcha's whole body arched up to his and her legs wrapped around his waist, taking him even deeper into a spiral of ecstasy too urgent and immediate to question. Driven by a force he'd never encountered before, Romain looked down into Sorcha's clear blue gaze, saw how her cheeks were hectic with colour, how she bit her lip to keep her moans back. He kissed her mouth to stop her biting it, unaware of the tender nature of his gesture.

And then he felt her bite his shoulder in direct response to the way her body was starting to contract around him—so powerfully that he could feel every spasm as it clenched around his shaft, urging him on to a deeper and more intense orgasm than he'd ever experienced. When it came, he actually blacked out for a second, and then the world came into focus again, his body still pulsing, still releasing.

After a long moment he pulled free and pulled Sorcha close into his chest, for that was the only thing he was capable of doing. And he knew in that moment that everything he'd thought or believed before had gone out of the window. But he was in no state to try and rationalise what that meant right now…

'I want to go home to Dublin, Romain. I have things to do there.'

Sorcha looked out of the window to the busy Paris street outside. Her whole body seemed to be one big, aching mass of fizzing nerve-ends. They'd made love all the previous evening and into the night. When she had commented on how Room Service had never arrived, Romain had informed her that he had asked that they were not to be disturbed. So then they had ordered Room Service again. And a bottle of wine.

As if too much personal history had been shared, they had been careful not to stray into those waters. They had spoken of general things, drunk the wine and eaten. And then afterwards they had made love again, long and languorously, until the dawn light had tinged the sky outside with pink.

He was dressing behind her. She could hear him pull up jeans, close the button, pull on his shirt… She closed her eyes and swallowed. Her body was reacting to just hearing him. God, she didn't even have to see him to want him. Her heart ached so much that it was like a physical pain.

The tenor of their relationship had changed so much since it had become physical. Romain was harder, more distant. The lightness that had existed between them, however briefly, at lunch that day in India was gone. Once he'd achieved what he'd set out to do the gloves had come off. And now the job was over and he was sating himself while he could. It was horrendously obvious. But though she knew *he* would be able to walk away, was used to this, she wouldn't. But she'd have to.

He came close behind her and she willed him away. But of course he didn't obey her silent plea. He pulled her hair aside at the back of her neck and pressed a kiss there, to the tender skin. A shudder of arousal ran through her. To stop it, she turned around.

'You *have* to come to the party. People will expect you to be there.'

'Romain, I—'

He felt a surge of anger move through him. Why did she have to be so stubborn?

'Sorcha, the job isn't officially over until after this party.'

She paled under his gaze, and he could see the shadows under her eyes. He felt his chest constrict. But something bigger motivated him, and he didn't want to look at what that was.

'Are you ordering me to go?' she asked quietly, her heart breaking a little more. Because, despite all the intimacy they'd shared, not one word of tenderness had been spoken. Even now, if he'd been asking her to come *with him*, because he wanted her there, then she would have gone without question. And castigated herself afterwards.

Romain stood stock still and thought silently to himself, *If that's what it takes.* Instead he shrugged. 'If you want to leave—leave. But you are expected to be there—to show a united front with myself, Zane…the rest of the board and the crew.'

She felt a little dead inside—cut off from everything around her. If she made a big deal and left, he might suspect something of her feelings for him. It would kill her to stay for one more night, but she would. Anything to avoid that penetrative gaze, that questioning mind.

She fixed her attention on something on the wall above his shoulder. 'Very well. There's an exhibition I wanted to see before I left. It won't make any huge difference if I leave tomorrow, I guess.'

Romain felt something suspiciously like relief flood him even as he reacted to her nonchalant tone.

'Good. I'll pick you up at seven.'

Big blue eyes caught his. 'I can go with—'

'*I'll* pick you up at seven.'

He pressed a swift kiss to her mouth, and she watched as he strode from the room.

The door shut behind him and Sorcha sank back onto the window seat behind her. For the first time since he'd arrived the evening before, her whole body sagged. Her mind was thankfully a little numb.

CHAPTER SIXTEEN

A LITTLE before seven that evening, Sorcha stood in much the same position as she had earlier, looking out of the window. She felt very still and serene inside, but she knew it was just the calm before the storm. The storm which was going to come when she would walk away from Romain and never see him again.

A knock sounded on the door and she jumped. That brief moment of tranquillity was gone. This evening was it—the last time she'd be with him, see him, experience him. So whatever fantasy she had in her head would have to be lived out tonight. She walked over to the door and opened it.

The breath left her body as if she *hadn't* already seen him in a tux—first in New York and now here again. She reacted as if it were the first time. He looked resplendent. Too gorgeous for words. His heavy-lidded sensuality was overwhelming.

Jerkily she gestured for him to come in. 'I just have to put on my shoes, then I'm good to go.'

She went into the small dressing room and pulled

out shoes from her open case. Coming back out into the bedroom, she saw he was looking at her strangely. She hopped from one foot to the other, pulling the shoes on. Not feeling like smiling at all, she managed to quirk a small one and ask, 'What's wrong? Have I got something on my nose?'

She went to look in the mirror, to check her reflection. Romain came and stood behind her, hands on her shoulders, and she could feel her body react just to that impersonal touch.

'You have no idea how stunning you are, do you?' he asked.

Sorcha blushed and tried to turn around, but he wouldn't let her. She refused to look at herself, mortified. 'Romain, I'm well aware that I'm lucky enough to have good genes that make me photogenic, but really there are a million women more stunning—'

He turned her almost savagely in his arms and tipped her chin up with a finger. 'You're the most beautiful woman I've ever seen.'

Inside and out.

She shook her head in denial. His mouth bent to hers, stopping any words. And when he broke away he whispered, 'Yes. You are.'

He reached into his pocket then and took something out—something in a long box. He flicked his eyes down to her shoes and his mouth quirked. 'This should match what you're wearing…'

Unaccustomed to receiving gifts from men, Sorcha didn't know what to do or say, so she took the box and opened it. A huge ruby glowed up at her from velvet folds like a living, breathing thing. Before she could articulate a word Romain had lifted it out and deftly fastened it. It hung on a long chain around her neck. Bare of any other jewellery, with her hair smoothed back behind her ears and falling down her back in a sleek black curtain, she did look perfect.

'Romain, I can't wear this. It must have cost a fortune.'

'Cost doesn't matter,' he dismissed arrogantly. 'Wear it for me. Please?'

She felt torn, all her instincts shouting at her to take it off. But she just gave a small nod.

He took her hand in his and led her from the room. She grabbed a small black bag and wrap as she went.

When they stood in the lift as it made its descent, Romain's eyes couldn't stray from Sorcha. He'd never seen her look more stunning. Her simple black silk dress had a deep vee halter neck, and was completely backless, showing off her pale skin, unblemished and silky smooth. It fell in soft swirling folds to her knees, and deep red, almost scarlet high heels added a splash of colour. But wasn't that her? She always surprised—never did the completely conventional thing. The ruby glowed and shone as it swayed with the movement of the lift, nestled between the firm globes of her breasts.

The trip to the venue for the party—a very well-known hotel right beside the Place de la Concorde—

was made largely in silence. The air that surrounded Sorcha seemed to hum with some indefinable energy. She was aware of Romain on the seat beside her, and his every minute movement seemed a thousand times bigger, more momentous. At one stage he reached across and took her hand. Pressed a kiss to the inside of her palm. It was the third time he'd kissed her like that, taking her breath away. To look into his eyes so deeply was torture, and yet she couldn't look away.

The car slid to a smooth halt and they got out, Romain helping her with a firm hand. Suddenly Sorcha was blinded by the sudden flashing of a thousand cameras. Shouts and incoherent questions were hurled their way.

'Romain—*Romain*!'

He hurried her through the crush and into the foyer, and when they got in she couldn't stop the uncontrollable shaking that had taken over her body. Those few seconds of flashing cameras had taken her back in time as if it was yesterday.

Romain made a gesture to someone that Sorcha didn't see, and led her over to a quiet corner. He sat her down on a seat and bent down on his haunches before her, looking up into her too pale face.

'Are you OK?'

She half nodded and shrugged, feeling his strength wrap itself around her. His two hands held hers and the heat was beginning to seep through, the chill leaving her body. She nodded again, more forcefully this time.

'I'm sorry. I just got a fright. I'm not used to that kind of reception—or at least I haven't been since…'

Romain looked grim. 'I'm sorry, I should have warned you. Come on, let's go inside. I'll get you a brandy.'

He pulled her up and, keeping a firm hold on her, walked her to the closed doors that led inside. For a second he stopped and looked down at her, to check if she was OK, and when he did she looked up at him. She gave a small smile and squeezed his hand gently, telling him what he needed to know with her eyes, and the sense of *déjà vu* that washed through him made stars dance in front of his eyes. This was the moment—*this* was what he'd been imagining in New York…

Sorcha, thinking he was waiting for her, tugged at his hand, and they went inside to a huge room which was already thronged with what looked like all of Paris. She wasn't aware of the slightly shell shocked look that had crossed Romain's face. She was fighting against the urge she had to sink into his side, clutch his hand for ever. She'd never had this level of protection before, and it felt far too seductive and irresistible. She had to remember that after tonight she wouldn't have it any more.

In the lavish ballroom, Romain didn't let Sorcha out of his protective sight. She chatted and joked with the crew, and other people she knew who'd been involved in the campaign, but her heart felt as heavy as a stone.

Some hours after arriving, close to the end of the

evening, Romain grabbed her hand in a fierce grip. She stifled a gasp and looked up to his face. He was ashen, and looking at something, or someone, she couldn't see.

'What is it?'

He didn't even seem to be aware that he was crushing her hand in his.

He muttered something unintelligible, and Sorcha asked again, 'Romain, what is it?'

'My brother,' he said, so faintly that she had to strain to hear him. 'My brother is here.'

Now she understood. She recalled what he had told her. Before Sorcha could speak again, or ask any questions, he muttered something, let her hand go and strode off into the throng.

Left alone for a moment, telling herself it was silly to feel so bereft, Sorcha went to the bar to get some water.

They had shown a rough cut of the commercial and Sorcha had to admit that it wasn't like anything out at the moment. It was whimsical and dreamy, and the shots from India looked fantastically exotic.

Sipping at the water, Sorcha turned when she felt a tap on her shoulder. A very beautiful blonde woman stood there, as tall as Sorcha, in a red gown which plunged daringly low, showing a more than generous cleavage. Sorcha could see immediately that she'd had work done—her face looked a little too perfect. Her eyes were blue, and glittered with a hard light.

Her red lips curved in an unfriendly smile, and Sorcha's own immediate smile faltered.

'You are Sorcha? The latest woman in Romain's life?'

Sorcha flushed deeply at the woman's rudeness, at the nerve she'd struck. She knew without doubt that she meant nothing good.

'I really don't see that that's any of your business.'

The other woman looked her up and down. 'Ah, but you see it is. Because if it wasn't for me you wouldn't be here tonight with him.'

Sorcha made a move to get away. Feeling as vulnerable as she did, the last thing she wanted was to deal with some ex-lover of Romain's.

The other woman stopped her by planting herself straight in front of Sorcha. Hemmed in by someone at her back, she couldn't move.

'Please excuse me.'

The woman arched a brow. 'You're not even curious as to who I might be?'

'Not really,' Sorcha answered, her eyes searching for and finding Romain. She found him easily enough. He was with a smaller man. They looked quite similar, and she realized that the man must be his brother. The other woman's face came close, and Sorcha could smell spirits on her breath. She shrank back.

'That man that he's with. That's his brother. My husband.'

Sorcha looked again, despite herself. The other

man's face was fleshy and mottled. She could see that from across the room. And middle age hadn't been kind to him. He had a definite paunch, and his hair was thinning on top.

'Not as handsome as Romain, is he?'

Sorcha flushed again, and tried to move.

'The ironic thing is, you see, I chose Marc over Romain. All those years ago Marc was the handsome one, the one with the prospects. As I'm sure you know, they had different fathers, so my full title is Duchesse de Courcy. Romain could only have offered me the title of Comtesse, and I was greedy…'

Sorcha went very still. The woman looked at Sorcha again, and utter hatred was in her eyes. Years of bitterness. Anger. Sorcha could see it a mile away—and she had an awful feeling she now knew exactly who she was.

'You…you were Romain's fiancée, weren't you?'

The woman laughed. 'He told you about me? How sweet. Did he tell you how heartbroken he was? How when he came in and found me on top of his brother he went white and proceeded to get blind drunk for a whole week?'

Sorcha was beginning to feel sick. But the woman was relentless.

'I ruined him for anyone else. *Me*. I may never have him now, but at least no one else will either—'

'Martine. Your husband is looking for you. I think it's time to leave.'

Romain materialised out of thin air and practically frogmarched Martine over to his brother. Someone escorted them out of the room.

On legs that felt none too steady, Sorcha went to find her bag and wrap. Two hands encircled her waist, bringing her back into contact with a hard, familiar body. She twisted around in his arms and looked up at him accusingly.

'You told me she was dead.' Hurt made her voice husky.

He shook his head. 'I said she was dead to me. I had no idea they would be here. But my brother heard about it on the grapevine and needed another hand-out…'

'That woman is poisonous, Romain. How could you have ever—?'

'Believe me, I ask myself that question every time I see her.' His face was carved from stone.

Sorcha felt cold inside. 'Your whole life, Romain…You do this…pursue beautiful women…it's all to get back at her, isn't it? Some sort of petty revenge?'

'Don't be crazy.'

Sorcha shook her head. Her insides were crumbling. 'It's not crazy. She said that because she'd rejected you, you wouldn't let anyone else have you—and it's true.'

Sorcha could feel the tension in his frame as he held her. His mouth was a slash of a line.

'Don't try to psychoanalyse me, Sorcha. And you're completely wrong. I look at that woman now and she fills me with disgust.'

'Yes, perhaps. But that doesn't stop how you allow her to keep affecting your behaviour.'

Her words hung in the air between them. They cut close to the bone. But Romain didn't want to poison the air with thoughts of Martine now. He pulled Sorcha close—close enough so that she could feel his arousal press against her.

Like a well trained mechanism, her body leapt into joyful response, totally going against the will her head was trying to impose on it.

One more night...that's all you have and then he'll move on. But for tonight he's yours...

Fighting an internal battle so strong that for one brief moment she thought she did have the strength to walk away, Sorcha quickly knew that her weak side had won out. The weak side that wanted, above all else, one more night with this man. So she allowed him to pull her even closer. And stared up into his eyes.

'Let's get out of here.'

The following morning, very early, Sorcha slid from the bed. Behind her, amongst the rumpled sheets, lay the languid and relaxed form of Romain's body. A sheet strategically hid the powerful centre of his manhood. His face looked younger in repose. Relaxed. Lashes curling darkly onto dark cheeks.

Sorcha's heart twisted so much in her chest that she almost made a sound. He shifted slightly and she held her breath. And then, when he didn't wake, stealthily she picked up her things and crept from his room back to her own, down the corridor…

CHAPTER SEVENTEEN

Two Weeks Later

'AND it's with great pleasure that I now declare this Dublin Youth Outreach Centre…' Sorcha bent and cut the blue ribbon over the door with a flourish '…open!'

It was amazing, really, she marvelled, how the human body and mind could conceal pain from everyone around them. Everyone was clapping and cheering, party poppers were going off, flashbulbs were flashing, TV cameras were whirring. This was a moment of great personal joy. She had done this single-handedly, with no help from anyone except herself—not even a penny from Tiarnan—so why was it all she could think about was the lonely ache in her heart?

'Sorcha, well done! You've done such a brilliant thing…and what a coup, getting the Prime Minister to launch it with you!'

Sorcha smiled as people filed past her into the centre, where the champagne was already flowing, giving their congratulations along the way. She'd got a call from Tiarnan that morning, to say good luck and that he was sorry he wouldn't be able to make it. Sorcha hadn't been surprised, but still it *hurt* that she had no one here to share this with her. Even Katie had had to cancel her flight at the last minute, as Maud had begged her to take on a job which, with her usual dramatics, had meant life or death.

She greeted the last person to go in. The news crews were packing up gear to bring it inside. So what if she was alone again?

Something across the road snagged her gaze… Sorcha's breath stopped right there in her throat as she watched a tall, dark man uncoil his body from a parked car across the road.

She had to be imagining things… Was she so distraught that she was hallucinating?

But as she blinked and watched it was unmistakably, without a doubt, Romain de Valois crossing the road. And the first thing that happened was that a huge lump in came to her throat. Of all her loved ones she'd want here, it had to be her *unrequited* love who came.

By the time he had crossed the road she had herself under some kind of control. When he stopped in front of her, she looked up and couldn't read his face. It was expressionless, and his eyes were hidden behind dark glasses, making him look even more mysterious, handsome. A dark suit and blue shirt made him look austere, formal. Her heart hammered like a piston.

He gestured with his head, as if he were looking her up and down behind those shades. 'Very demure...for a woman who leaves a man in the middle of the night without even a note.'

His voice and that accent caused such an immediate reaction in her blood that she almost swayed. He must be referring to her outfit. She'd dressed relatively conservatively today, knowing that some elements of the press would be out to get her. In a grey pencil skirt, white high-necked blouse, her hair tied back in a ponytail and her glasses on, her only concession to fashion or frivolity were the black fishnet tights and eye-wateringly high black heels.

Her chin tipped up, her eyes clear, belying the whirlpool her stomach had become. 'It was the morning, actually, and I thought you'd prefer a clean break.'

One brow arched up. 'Oh, did you, now? How considerate.'

He took the glasses off and finally she could see his eyes. But they too were cool, expressionless. Even so, joy at seeing him again ripped through her and held her captive. She hoped the extra make-up she'd had to put on covered the shadows under her eyes. She was so pale she couldn't get away with anything.

'Now is not the time or place to discuss your leaving. I believe you have a speech to give?'

Her speech!

She'd forgotten everything—where she was, what she was doing.

Romain took her lightly under the elbow and led her into the centre, where everyone was chatting loudly. The TV crews had set up and were indeed waiting patiently for her to speak. Nerves threatened to attack her, and for a brief moment Romain wasn't the centre of her universe. But knowing that he was there emboldened her. She didn't care about how or why he was there—just drew on his strength because she needed someone.

When she stood up, her voice faltered at first. But then she saw Romain at the back of the room. He nodded at her, telling her without words that she was OK, that she could do this. And she did. She made a very impassioned speech, telling a little of her own history, how lost she'd felt as a young person. There was a long moment of silence when she finished, and then huge, raucous applause.

For some time afterwards she was swept into interviews and photos and conversations. And every time she looked for Romain she saw him chatting to someone different. He wasn't brooding in a corner, as she might have expected. At one point she looked over and he was throwing his head back, laughing at something someone had said. It made her heart swell and soar.

And she had to be very careful. Because if he had come just to pick up their physical relationship, then she wasn't interested. And she was quite sure he wasn't interested in anything else.

* * *

'So. What *are* you doing here?'

They were walking out of the centre. It had turned dark outside. Sorcha's heels sounded loud in the quiet of the empty city street.

He didn't answer. 'I'll give you a lift home.'

'You don't know where I live.'

'You should know by now that I know everything.'

Sorcha gave in wearily. His arrogance was by now wholly usual. He led her to his car and, much to her chagrin, he did know exactly where she lived. He drove there as if he knew the city better than herself. When she got out, he got out too, and followed her to her door. She turned as she slid the key in the lock.

'Look, if you've come here just to—'

'I've come here to talk to you.'

Silly flutters made her heart jump, and she furiously clamped them down. He was probably peeved that she'd walked out without saying goodbye, that was all.

When they got up to her apartment, which was at the top of the house, she realised that she'd never had a man in her flat before. Or at least not a *lover*. She felt self-conscious at the thought of him seeing her inner sanctum, and busied herself turning on lamps and going into the kitchen, opening and closing doors. She turned around to ask him what he'd prefer and he was right behind her, holding two bottles of beer.

'But how did you…?'

'One in each pocket. I know you don't like champagne, and I knew you'd want to celebrate today…'

Stupidly, Sorcha felt tears threaten. She reached up and pinched her nose, taking off her glasses on the pretext of cleaning them. Romain put the beers down and took her glasses out of her hands, tipping her face to his.

Her eyes were swimming, her throat working and her lips trembling. It was all he could to not to take them, touch his lips to hers…but now was not the time. Instead he pulled her into his chest and held her tight, rocking her as she wept and made his shirt wet.

After a while Sorcha pulled back, feeling silly. Two minutes in her apartment and she was weeping all over Romain like some hormonal teenager. She avoided his eyes, knowing she must have mascara everywhere. She rubbed at her cheeks and her eyes felt raw and puffy. 'I'm sorry. I don't know what came over me.'

'It's OK,' he said gently. 'You felt lonely. I know, because I've felt like that for a long time.'

She looked up at him warily and rubbed at her cheeks. 'You?'

He nodded and took her hands away, rubbing at her cheeks with his thumbs, his big hands around her jaw.

His voice was husky. 'I'm very proud of what you did today.'

'You are?' she said, knowing she must sound like some kind of parrot. She was completely bemused and confused as to why he was here, what he wanted.

He nodded and, taking the beers, led her out into

the sitting room, making her sit down. He expertly flipped open the beer tops and shucked off his overcoat, sitting down beside her. His scent, his presence, overwhelmed her, and Sorcha took a big swig of beer just to try and counteract the shock.

'Why did you leave like that, Sorcha?' His eyes pinned her to the spot.

Feeling agitated, she stood up. Somewhere between the door and the kitchen she had kicked off her shoes. She hugged her arms around her and went to stand by the window. She firmed her inner resolve. 'Because I thought you'd prefer it like that.'

She couldn't help but recall how close she had been to turning around and going back. It had been at that moment, in the cab, on the way to the airport, that she had noticed the morning paper. A photo of her and Romain, leaked from God knew where had been splashed across the front page. Her in his arms on the beach on Inis Mor. And inside more pictures of him with ex-lovers, and the one of him dining with Solange Colbert. And a huge discussion about which woman was the new one in his life, and the pros and cons for each. It had been hideous. And it had made it very easy for Sorcha to keep going straight to the airport.

'And what gave you that impression?' He sat back, as at home as if he lived there, one arm across the back of the couch. Relaxed. Debonair. Disconcerting to her equilibrium.

Suddenly Sorcha felt angry at the way he'd

swanned back into her life, threatening to turn it upside down all over again. She conveniently blocked out the fact that she'd only felt half alive for the past two weeks.

'Oh, I don't know, Romain! Maybe it's something to do with the fact that you have a reputation that would make Casanova blush… I mean, what *did* you want?' She threw her arms wide.

He stood and was immediately dangerous. 'You, Sorcha. I wanted you and I still want you. I decided to give you the benefit of the doubt. I would have thought, Well, she must do this with every lover. But I knew that I had been your first—so unless you're planning a lifetime of having sex and walking away then maybe it's not something that came so easily.'

His words flayed her. This was it. This was where she had to protect herself. He was advancing, and she knew that if he so much as breathed near her she'd turn to mush. So she squared her shoulders and said cuttingly, 'Well, that's exactly it. You *were* my first lover, Romain, but I don't expect you to be my last. So if it's closure you're looking for, then this is it. I meant to leave you like that. I knew it was coming to an end. You obviously didn't.'

And somehow, as if invaded by some alien force, she kept going, the words spilling out in a stream of consciousness, all designed to protect herself. 'Was it because it happened to you? You had your heart broken by the person you entrusted your secrets to? So you felt bad for me—wanted to make sure I was all right? Well, I'm fine. You can see I'm fine. Now, please, if all you wanted was to salve your conscience I'll save you the bother, because I'm fine.'

Romain looked as if she had just slapped him in the face. His mouth compressed to a thin line of anger.

'You said "I'm fine" three times. I get the point. I'm not welcome.'

He picked up his coat and carefully, too carefully, put it over his arm.

Sorcha was already feeling the effects of her words on her body. An out-of-control shaking starting up in her legs.

Romain turned and walked to the door. Sorcha's vision blurred, and for a second she thought she'd faint.

He turned then and looked at her. Through her. He smiled, but it was harsh and didn't meet his eyes. 'Do you know the really funny thing? I've let history repeat itself. All these years I've been so careful to avoid getting emotionally involved...and within minutes of meeting you in New York, when I knew you were tempted to throw that champagne in my face, I was already more emotionally involved with you than I'd ever been with anyone in my life. When I woke up that morning two weeks ago and realised you had gone—*left*...the pain was indescribable. The only thing that gave me the courage to come here today was a misguided belief that I had seen something in your eyes that might lead me to believe...'

He shook his head and opened the door.

Sorcha couldn't move she was in so much shock.

Before leaving he turned back one more time and smiled sadly. 'It would appear that I am destined to play the fool in love. For you, Sorcha, have my heart—whether you like it or not. Perhaps that's my punishment for judging you so cruelly—not once, but twice. I didn't lose my heart to Martine all those years ago. It took seeing her with you in the same room that night to realise that. All I lost was my head and my pride. But this...*this* is much worse, and I can see exactly why I protected myself for so long if not being loved brings this level of pain. *Adieu*, Sorcha, I hope you find happiness and love in your life.'

When he had gone, and the door had clicked quietly shut behind him, Sorcha's hands went to her mouth as she stifled a sob that wouldn't emerge. She was frozen. Couldn't move. She heard the main door slam. She heard a car door open. Close. And finally she was galvanised into action. She didn't think, she moved. Like lightning. Sprinting down the stairs, taking two at a time, until she got to the heavy front door. She was all fingers and thumbs opening it, but finally it sprang free.

The rain had arrived. It was lashing. She saw Romain's car pulling out of the parking space, into the road, about to drive off.

'No!' she shouted, her voice hoarse with emotion. 'Romain...come back...*come back!*'

He started to drive away, and Sorcha ran down the

steps in her stockinged feet, heedless of the rain and the wet pavement. She had to hitch up her skirt in order to run after his car.

'Romain, wait! *Wait!*'

The car was driving away, too far, too fast, and she faltered, her steps slowing, a sob rising. It was too late. Already she was thinking of what she could do—where she could go to find him, track him down, Maud must know where he lived—and then she saw that the car had stopped, red brake lights on.

Almost hesitant to walk forward, in case he sped off again, Sorcha walked tentatively. When she saw that he wasn't going anywhere she sped up and ran the last few feet. She pulled open his door. She was saturated, hair plastered to her head, clothes stuck to her. Rain ran in rivulets down her face.

She was crying, big racking sobs, tears mingling with the rain on her face.

'You big idiot. Of course I love you. I love you so much I can't eat, sleep or think. The only reason I left that morning was because you gave me no indication that I meant anything to you except an a…a…affair. You said you just wanted a mistress…'

He stepped out of the car and she thumped him on his shoulder. He wrapped his arms around her waist so tight that she couldn't breathe and lifted her up, feet off the ground, head buried in her neck. She pressed kisses wherever she could find a spot, and when he could he pulled back and let her down gently. The rain coursed over them but they were oblivious. He grabbed her close again and drove his mouth down onto hers, taking and giving no quarter, passionately demanding her promise again, and she gave it, stretching up, her whole body arching into his.

'God, Sorcha…' he breathed finally when he lifted his head, his breath coming harsh and swift. 'Don't ever do that to me again.'

She hit him again on the shoulder. 'Well, don't shut me out again.'

He smiled. 'Deal.'

And then he got down on one knee, still oblivious to the weather. Sorcha felt her heart about to burst from her chest.

Romain looked up, so heartrendingly tender that she caught her breath. 'I just got you a temporary ring for now…on the way over here. I didn't want to tempt fate by getting the real thing, and I know you'd probably like to choose it yourself anyway…'

Sorcha smiled and hiccupped as he took her hand.

'Will you please marry me and make me a sane man, before I go crazy with love for you?'

She nodded immediately. He held out a cheap silver Claddagh ring, and Sorcha thought she'd never seen anything more lovely. He slid it onto her finger and she looked at it. She held out her hand to him. It was shaking.

'It's on the wrong way.'

'What?'

'If we're…' she looked down at him shyly, 'In

love the heart should be facing my heart, and even on this finger, some might consider us already married.'

He stood up and took the ring off her finger, carefully turning it round so that when he slid it on again the heart faced inwards.

'Then as of this moment and until we make it official, we are married. You have my heart... always.'

'As you have mine,' she promised, gazing up into his eyes, her hand tracing his jaw.

He bent his head again and kissed her, long and deeply, and it was only the honking of a horn that broke them apart. An irate taxi driver was waiting behind Romain's still running car, his head sticking out of the window.

'Would the two of you just get a room?'

Much later, as the moonlight broke through stormy clouds outside and bathed Sorcha's room with milky light, she held Romain's head to her breast and stroked his hair.

'You know...' he said musingly, as his hand ran up and down her arm.

'Hmm...' she said, too blissfully tired to make it a question.

'When I stopped the car that time, I hadn't seen you behind me. I stopped because I was determined to come back and make you see that you loved me, whether you liked it or not. It was killing me to think that I had been your first lover and yet you wanted to experience others, so I was going to come back and make love to you till you begged for mercy. Then you appeared at my door, soaking, like an avenging angel, telling me you loved me. I thought I was dreaming…'

'So you mean I went out there and ruined my tights and got soaking wet for nothing?'

He flipped up and hovered over her, his big body gleaming in the light, his eyes blazing into hers, telling her of his love.

'But it was fun drying off…no?'

She twined her hands around his neck, 'Oh, yes…that was definitely fun…'

They kissed long and luxuriously.

'You know, I want lots of children, with jet-black hair and blue eyes,' Romain said as he kissed his way down Sorcha's neck.

Joy surged through her.

'I think blue is a recessive gene to grey.'

'Not in our children,' Romain declared arrogantly.

Sorcha shook her head and smiled fondly. 'No, they wouldn't dare.'

He came over her then, imprisoning her body with his, making her very aware of his newly aroused state. Sorcha's hair rippled onto the pillow behind her like black silk. Her cheeks were flushed. Her eyes were slumberous, like a cat's. Romain realised that this was the exact image he'd had in his head all those weeks ago in Dublin, the day she'd walked out of the restaurant. As confident as he had been then that he could make it come true, he hadn't counted on the journey it would take him on, or the wealth of experience this woman would bring into his life, enriching him emotionally beyond anything he could have ever dreamed. He felt love surge through him again. Strong and true.

He smoothed the back of his hand across one flushed cheek and smiled down into blue eyes darkened with passion, burning with love.

Sorcha locked her arms behind his head, bringing her breasts up and into close contact with his chest. She looked serious. 'Romain…you do know I couldn't give two hoots about becoming a countess, or the château…or anything? All I care about is you… I love *you*…'

He sank into those blue depths. He'd truly found the one person in the world who loved *him*…who knew him completely. As he knew her.

'I know…' he said huskily.

'Good.' She smiled cheekily. 'Then hurry up and make love to me. I'm not getting any younger, and if you want lots of babies…'

'It would be my pleasure…for ever.'

And it was.

* * * * *

*Look for LAST WOLF WATCHING
by Rhyannon Byrd—
the exciting conclusion in the
BLOODRUNNERS miniseries
from Silhouette Nocturne.*

*Follow Michaela and Brody on their fierce journey
to find the truth and face the demons from the past,
as they reach the heart of the battle between the
Runners and the rogues.*

*Here is a sneak preview of book three,
LAST WOLF WATCHING.*

Michaela squinted, struggling to see through the impenetrable darkness. Everyone looked toward the Elders, but she knew Brody Carter still watched her. Michaela could feel the power of his gaze. Its heat. Its strength. And something that felt strangely like anger, though he had no reason to have any emotion toward her. Strangers from different worlds, brought together beneath the heavy silver moon on a night made for hell itself. That was their only connection.

The second she finished that thought, she knew it was a lie. But she couldn't deal with it now. Not tonight. Not when her whole world balanced on the edge of destruction.

Willing her backbone to keep her upright, Michaela Doucet focused on the towering blaze of a roaring bonfire that rose from the far side of the clearing, its orange flames burning with maniacal zeal against the inky black curtain of the night. Many of the Lycans had already shifted into their preternatural shapes, their fur-covered bodies standing like monstrous shadows at the edges of the forest as they waited with restless expectancy for her brother.

Her nineteen-year-old brother, Max, had been attacked by a rogue werewolf—a Lycan who preyed upon humans for food. Max had been bitten in the attack, which meant he was no longer human, but a breed of creature that existed between the two worlds of man and beast, much like the Bloodrunners themselves.

The Elders parted, and two hulking shapes emerged from the trees. In their wolf forms, the Lycans stood over seven feet tall, their legs bent at an odd angle as they stalked forward. They each held a thick chain that had been wound around their inside wrists, the twin lengths leading back into the shadows. The Lycans had taken no more than a few steps when they jerked on the chains, and her brother appeared.

Bound like an animal.

Biting at her trembling lower lip, she glanced left, then right, surprised to see that others had joined her. Now the Bloodrunners and their family and friends stood as a united force against the Silvercrest pack, which had yet to accept the fact that something sinister was eating away at its foundation—something that would rip down the protective walls that separated their world from the humans'. It occurred to Michaela that loyalties were being announced tonight—a separation made between those who would stand with the Runners in their fight against the rogues and those who blindly supported the pack's refusal to face reality. But all she could focus on was her brother. Max looked so hurt…so terrified.

"Leave him alone," she screamed, her soft-soled, black satin slip-ons struggling for purchase in the damp earth as she rushed toward Max, only to find herself lifted off the ground when a hard, heavily muscled arm clamped around her waist from behind, pulling her clear off her feet. "Damn it, let me down!" she snarled, unable to take her eyes off her brother as the golden-eyed Lycan kicked him.

Mindless with heartache and rage, Michaela clawed at the arm holding her, kicking her heels against whatever part of her captor's legs she could reach. "Stop it," a deep, husky voice grunted in her ear. "You're not helping him by losing it. I give you my word he'll survive the ceremony, but you have to keep it together."

"Nooooo!" she screamed, too hysterical to listen to reason. "You're monsters! All of you! Look what you've done to him! How dare you! *How dare you!*"

The arm tightened with a powerful flex of muscle, cinching her waist. Her breath sucked in on a sharp, wailing gasp.

"Shut up before you get both yourself and your brother killed. I will *not* let that happen. Do you understand me?" her captor growled, shaking her so hard that her teeth clicked together. "Do you understand me, Doucet?"

"Damn it," she cried, stricken as she watched one of the guards grab Max by his hair. Around them Lycans huffed and growled as they watched the spectacle, while others outright howled for the show to begin.

"That's enough!" the voice seethed in her ear. "They'll tear you apart before you even reach him, and I'll be damned if I'm going to stand here and watch you die."

Suddenly, through the haze of fear and agony and outrage in her mind, she finally recognized who'd caught her. *Brody*.

He held her in his arms, her body locked against his powerful form, her back to the burning heat of his chest. A low, keening sound of anguish tore through her, and her head dropped forward as hoarse sobs of pain ripped from her throat. "Let me go. I have to help him. *Please*," she begged brokenly, knowing only that she needed to get to Max. "Let me go, Brody."

He muttered something against her hair, his breath warm against her scalp, and Michaela could have sworn it was a single word…. But she must have heard wrong. She was too upset. Too furious. Too terrified. She must be out of her mind.

Because it sounded as if he'd quietly snarled the word *never*.

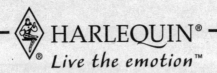

HARLEQUIN®
Live the emotion™

American ROMANCE®

Heart, Home & Happiness

HARLEQUIN®

Blaze™

Red-hot reads.

HARLEQUIN®

EVERLASTING LOVE™

Every great love has a story to tell™

HH Harlequin® Historical
Historical Romantic Adventure!

HARLEQUIN®

HARLEQUIN ROMANCE®

From the Heart, For the Heart

HARLEQUIN®

INTRIGUE®

Breathtaking Romantic Suspense

Medical Romance™...
love is just a heartbeat away

N_ext™

**There's the life you planned.
And there's what comes next.**

HARLEQUIN®
Presents®

Seduction and Passion Guaranteed!

HARLEQUIN®

Super Romance®

Exciting, Emotional, Unexpected

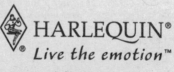

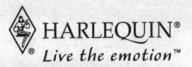

HARLEQUIN®
INTRIGUE®

BREATHTAKING ROMANTIC SUSPENSE

Shared dangers and passions lead to electrifying romance and heart-stopping suspense!

Every month, you'll meet six new heroes who are guaranteed to make your spine tingle and your pulse pound. With them you'll enter into the exciting world of Harlequin Intrigue— where your life is on the line and so is your heart!

THAT'S INTRIGUE— ROMANTIC SUSPENSE AT ITS BEST!

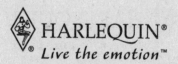

HARLEQUIN®
Live the emotion™

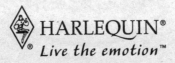

Harlequin® Historical
Historical Romantic Adventure!

Imagine a time of chivalrous knights and unconventional ladies, roguish rakes and impetuous heiresses, rugged cowboys and spirited frontierswomen—— these rich and vivid tales will capture your imagination!

Harlequin Historical... they're too good to miss!

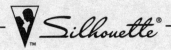

SPECIAL EDITION™

Emotional, compelling stories that capture the intensity of living, loving and creating a family in today's world.

Modern, passionate reads that are powerful and provocative.

nocturne

Dramatic and sensual tales of paranormal romance.

Romances that are sparked by danger and fueled by passion.